THE RIDE

Nancy Cathers Demme

STEPHEN F. AUSTIN STATE UNIVERSITY PRESS

For more information:
Stephen F. Austin State University Press
P.O. Box 13007 SFA Station
Nacogdoches, Texas 75962
sfapress@sfasu.edu
www.sfasu.edu/sfapress

Project Manager: Kimberly Verhines
Book design by Sarah Johnson
Cover art and chapter illustrations: Tristan Brewser

ISBN: 978-1-62288-473-5

Acknowledgments

A round of applause goes out to my editor, Sarah D. Johnson, who has navigated my passage with kind good humor and knowledge. A heartfelt thanks goes out to the late, Don Lasko, whose critical contributions were never taken with a grain of salt. John Langendoerfer, Edith McGowan, Hedda Colossi, Tony Athmejar, Beverly Geller, and Sophia Chrysoulakis continue to be inspiration and impetus. Long felt admiration goes to Donald Woodbridge, Linda Caffrey, and Barbara Hammer who shared their time and expertise and friendship. The chorus of storytellers at the Garden State Storytellers' League were instrumental for their continued encouragement and confidence in my work. To Lawrence Mansier I pledge my eternal gratitude for catapulting me on this wonderful journey. Lastly I would like to thank Travis, Scott, Wendy and Kris whose lifelong belief in me has never wavered.

"and I think I know how a soul feels when it sees its body buried in the ground and lost."

—John Steinbeck,
The Pastures of Heaven

1952 El Paso

Chapter 1:
Ralph Preston

All he knew was America, the parched grass, the flooding rains when they came, the tornadoes, Tex Mex. He knew nothing of the Sierra Madre de Chiapas of his grandfathers. He was fifteen, anonymous. His stepfather mucked stalls on a ranch. His mother cooked rice and beans, rice and beans, over and over again. His sisters giggled then sulked. Not to arouse suspicion he decided on short hops, El Paso to Odessa. He had stolen a map from the gas station, not knowing they were free and had hidden it in his pants where it crackled every time he took a step. He felt in his pocket for the Diamond Tips. He had not meant to bring them. He had taken the twenty dollars his mother stored in a coffee tin, dimes and pennies, nickels, her life savings.

Diego Ramírez noticed things, the fecundity of grasses, the age of wood, the brilliance of the unwavering sun, but he was unsure how to hitchhike. He had been picked up numerous times from the men working the ranch, on his way to school, and then as he made his way back. But this was different. He had a choice. He would choose a small blue sedan, a red sports car, maybe a roaring

Mac. He sat alongside the highway twirling tall grasses between his palms until they slipped back to earth as dust. It was still dark. He would not hitchhike until dawn. He stood and started walking east, trying to put as much distance from El Paso as he could. The burlap sack was heavy with his coins.

He had wrapped them in a paper sack and tied them with twine so they would not jingle, but with each step, he heard them breaking loose and rattling the predawn quiet. Animals skittered into the brush as he walked, but he was not afraid. He was running, and it felt good. Cars roared past in the night, their headlights making the growth along the road stark and ghostlike. A thin line of light shrouded by a cloudy grey umbrella seized the horizon. Diego turned to the west, from where he had come, and a white Mac truck screamed toward him. He faced the oncoming truck with his arm thrust out, but the truck raced past. He worried that he did not get the ride because he did not use his thumb. He refused to use his thumb. That was a tool for boys. He was a man.

As the sun slowly rose, he picked up stray pieces of paper caught in the brush, newspaper, bits of letters, pages from books. He carefully put them in his sack to decipher later. He read haphazardly, recognizing some words but not others. He mouthed the letters, and they would escape his lips like a mournful kiss.

The sun was well up, blanching everything in its path, making it hard for him to look east. The horizon was a stark shimmer, so he turned west and walked backwards looking eagerly now for oncoming traffic. Little beads of sweat sprang from the back of his neck as the sun scorched his back. He was shamed for not thinking to steal his stepfather's precious thermos and fill it with the sweet *café con leche*. His tongue, thick in his mouth, clucked at himself disapprovingly for being foolish.

It was still early, and traffic was sparse. *There will be rides*, he thought nervously, but his arm had grown heavy, and he stumbled over gravel in his backward march. He had walked far from El Paso in three hours, up before dawn, before his mother's bustling, before his stepfather's bark. He was to start work at the Circle

Q this morning. His stepfather had arranged it. He was to walk each of the thirty horses each day. If he was good, his stepfather promised, if the ranch boss liked his work, he would not have to return to the school in the fall, to the big rambling school where a Mexican boy would get lost, the high school. This was the plan his stepfather had mapped for him. Diego had been put back a grade twice already, and the plan was set. It did not matter that Diego was terrified of horses, of their menacing hooves, and their large, twisting necks and snapping teeth. He did not find them beautiful, as his stepfather had, or as work beasts as the ranch boss did. Diego ground his teeth, much like the horses he feared, when a red semi slowed and stopped on the narrow spit of gravel before him.

"You don't need school Diego," his stepfather had bellowed. "You need me. Me!" and he had thumped his chest with his thumb.

A big beefy hand clamped onto the open window on Diego's side. The hand was brown, and black hairs glistened in the sun.

"You looking for a ride?" a voice called, and the hand disappeared, and then the passenger door opened. "You looking for a ride?"

"I guess so," Diego said with a sad finality.

"Then climb in. I have to be in Dallas today." The man was white, pink really, bald with a tuft of wispy white hair sprouting from his neck, his left arm brown where he held it outside of the window.

As Diego climbed with difficulty up into the passenger seat, he noticed with lowered eyes, the man's porcine belly, the western shirt, once white but weathered to grey, spattered with gravy stains.

Suddenly the man clenched Diego's chin. "How old are you?"

"Eighteen."

"By God, all you Mexicans look like kids," and he released his hold roughly. The truck vibrated with Diego's silence. The man put the truck in gear, looked in his rearview mirror, and chugged out onto the highway. When the truck had gained some momentum, he asked, "Where are you going?"

"Odessa."

"Odessa? Had a wife once was from there. Never lived there mind you, but I can tell you that Delia never let up on how it was so divine. Said her parents raised her Christian. You're Catholic I suppose."

"Yes, Sir."

"Never could figure how folks got so wound up in that hocus pocus," he said, his meaty arms steering the wheel around a curve. "Christians tell you straight, you learn or you burn. Delia was one of those burning types. Couldn't stand me being on the road. Said she was lonely. She was lonely all right," and he looked out again at his mirror. "Christian bah. She was raised about as Christian as a locust. What's your business in Odessa?"

"My father lives there."

"Then what are you doing in El Paso?"

"My mother is there."

The bald man poked Diego in the ribs. "Could be she's a bit like Delia. Quick to burn, slow to learn."

"She's a seamstress. Her business is there. My father is in Odessa."

"One of those sad stories?"

"No, not really. They see each other."

"On occasion, if you get my meaning."

Diego did not get his meaning. He did not know the word 'occasion.' He fought not to open the door and fling himself to the road. Suddenly the bald man stuck out his hand.

"Ralph Preston," and he took Diego's hand and shook it. "You. Your name?"

"Pedro Gómez."

"Well, I'm pleased to meet you," and he turned up the radio to loud country music that drowned out the roar of the engine.

After his long trek in the morning heat, Diego teetered on the edge of sleep, rising and falling. The music rolled and twisted, like a storm out on the Rio Grande, but then a loud cry would come from the radio, and he would bolt upright. A pack of Lucky Strikes and an open matchbook rested on the dashboard. Diego was tempted to pocket them when the driver turned to look out the side mirror. Sand and dirt littered the floor in front of him. Papers fluttered on a clipboard. A thermos jiggled in the box between them. The driver had a dragon tattoo with a crimson heart emblazoned on his arm. Diego reached out with his finger as if to trace it when Ralph Preston boomed.

"You like barbecue?" he shouted, turning the volume down on the radio.

Diego's mouth watered at the mere mention. "Yes, Sir, I do," he replied, though he had only stood outside the barbecue houses.

"Best barbecue's in Odessa. A sweet little place, you'd never suspect. I'm hungry just thinking about it."

Diego wished he had never mentioned it. The rice and beans he had pilfered from his mother's leftovers had long since filled him.

"Best sweet potato pie, too. Did you bring any money?"

"No," he lied.

"I'll stake you some when we get there. You won't regret it."

They had hours to go before they got to Odessa. Diego was slavering already.

"Do you have sisters?"

"Two sisters."

"Pretty I bet. The Mexican girls are always pretty with those black eyes that see into the dark. Pretty. What are their names?"

Diego didn't want to say their true names. He wanted to keep the driver in the dark, but he couldn't think of other names quickly enough. "Esmerelda," he whispered.

"What's that again?"

"Esmerelda," Diego said irritably. There was no cause to bring them into this, into this truck with a man with a dragon tattoo.

"Mexican names always mean something. What does Esmerelda mean?"

"Green stone. I don't know."

"I could'a guessed. Smooth pretty. I bet she's the prettiest?"

"She is," Diego lied again. Esmerelda was thin and bony. Her face reminded him of a hawk with a disposition to match.

"The other?"

"Almira. She's pretty, too, small like a rabbit compared to Esmerelda."

"That's the one I want to meet. I like my women small—had a date once with a midget. I will never forget that as long as I live. She broke it off before it started, saying I was too big for her. Funny. I've never forgotten it to this day. I was drunk as a skunk for two days after, but I never forgot." Ralph Preston got quiet as if he had downed too many beers. "Maybe you could introduce us. When we get to Odessa, maybe you could introduce your sister."

"Sure, sure," Diego cooed, feeling as if he had a handle on these things. "But she's in El Paso. Maybe next trip."

"My luck." Silence grew between them, and music twanged sadly. "I saw you looking at this," and Ralph Preston stroked his arm. "She's a beauty, ain't she? Got it done years ago in a little tattoo parlor with a brothel in back. More for your buck."

"What's the red heart mean?"

"Passion. I'm a man full of passion. It's why I drive this rig," he said, pounding the steering wheel with his fist. "It's mine you know. I'm a rogue carrier. Work for myself. The way I like."

"What're you carrying?"

"Potatoes. Russet. Thousands of pounds of them. Delivery Dallas. I'll have to drive like hell to get them there first thing tomorrow." He motioned to the thermos. "You want a swig?"

"No thanks," he said, his tongue stuck to the roof of his mouth. "It's a fine tattoo."

"The girls like it. Since I got that thing, I got more special feeling in that arm than in the other if you know what I mean?"

"Sure," Diego whispered.

"I'm gonna open up this thing. Make some time. Hold on."

The rig lurched and caught and sped faster.

"Close your window 'til there's just a crack open; otherwise there's too much drag."

Diego closed his window until a thin stream of air passed through. He thought he might be sick from the speed and the bumps on the road, the swift passing of smaller vehicles, the heat. He wanted to sleep, and he pushed his body into the door and rested his head on his burlap sack. He wanted to tell Ralph Preston that he was going to sleep, that he didn't want to talk about his sisters, or potatoes, or tattoos. When he finally fell asleep, he dreamed of barbecue.

He awoke to Ralph Preston's gruff voice calling him.

"Pedro! Pedro! Look alive. We're here. The barbecue center of the world is waiting. Wake!"

Diego didn't know Pedro. He had forgotten him in the sweet dreams of barbecue. He didn't remember the fire, but his nostrils burned with the grey scent of ash. Then as Ralph Preston called for Pedro again, he sat up, straight up, his face hot with flame, and remembered where he was.

They were in Odessa before a squat brown building, the letters BAR-B-Q painted across a grimy window. Ralph Preston's big rig took up most of the narrow street.

"This is heaven," Ralph Preston said as he climbed out of the truck. "Pedro, we're here. You coming?"

"I'm here," Diego said groggily. Even before he climbed out of the cab, he could smell pork simmering, and his mouth watered.

Ralph Preston held the torn screen door open for him. "You have just met paradise. Hey, Emil," Ralph Preston called, coming into the dark room.

Emil was a cowboy chef, scuffed cowboy boots, a short-sleeved red-fringed shirt, muscles bulging, a wooden spoon in one upraised hand. "You're back this way?"

"Couldn't resist. I'm in heaven just smelling. Meet Pedro Gómez," he said, pushing Diego forward. "This is his birthday. We want the works."

Diego nodded solemnly to the cowboy. He had never been in a restaurant before. He inhaled the sweet and savory. This is not his mother's rice and beans, he thought. He looked to Ralph Preston for what to do. His burlap sack dragged along the floor.

"You might want to wash up," Emil said, motioning to a

narrow hallway with his spoon. He winked at Ralph.

"Yeah, you go on. It's back there. Soap and water, Pedro. You sabe?" As Diego walked toward the hallway, Ralph Preston called, "Hombre." Diego turned to stare at him.

Diego thought he must make the right choice as he made his way down the hallway. One door was emblazoned with a bull, the other a cow. *Hombre*, yes, *hombre*.

Diego could barely turn around in the tiny bathroom. He gazed into the large mirror, unlike the cracked mirror at home, the one his stepfather had broken in a fit of rage. He stared deeply into his own brown eyes. The ride had changed him. He looked more guarded, chiseled, more like Pedro Gómez than Diego Ramirez. He took the grey bar of soap and turned on the faucet, his eyes still locked on his reflection. He tore a paper towel from the rack and scrubbed his neck and chest until he smelled less like mesquite and chili powder.

When Ralph Preston took his turn in the bathroom, Diego was alone with the cowboy. He knew cowboys, dark, moody, somber men or men quick to explosive laughter. Watching the cowboy stir his barbecue, Diego thought he might be the laughter type. The cowboy looked up, "You cook?"

"No."

"Who cooks for you. A senorita?" he said smiling.

"My Mama."

"Ah, Mama. What's her specialty?"

Diego didn't know *specialty*. He quickly looked away.

"What's her best meal?"

"Rice and beans." Diego knew *best*.

"Well, you won't be getting any rice and beans today. Potatoes in garlic and pork barbecue is on the menu. Hope you won't mind?"

"No, Sir. I don't mind."

Ralph Preston reappeared, slapped Diego's back, and barked, "I'm as ready as if I were a virgin. Let's get on with it."

The cowboy handed two steaming platters over the counter.

They each took one and then sat at a small, square table. Diego sat before his plate, his hands folded, waiting for supper prayers. Ralph Preston already had the sandwich in his mouth, sauce dripping down his mouth to his chin.

"Dig in, Pedro."

But Diego couldn't. His mother had always been full of prayers, prayers for the leaky roof, prayers for the broken mirror, prayers for food. This meal deserved a long grace, and while Diego's eyes rolled back in his head at the heavenly smells, he silently mouthed a prayer fit for a saint. Then he lifted his sandwich and let the hickory sauce roll over his tongue.

"Good, huh?" Ralph Preston asked.

Diego couldn't speak. He was transported to another world. Nothing had ever tasted this good. He ate in silence. The potatoes were hot and sharp with garlic. Ralph Preston squirted some ketchup from a plastic bottle onto Diego's plate.

"Dunk the potatoes."

Tentatively Diego dipped a potato into the red sauce. The world couldn't get better. He liked Pedro Gómez. It had been wise to run. They ate the rest of the meal in silence, both afraid to test the spell the food had over them. Ralph Preston slapped his napkin on the table, rocked back on his chair, and belched. "Better than ever," he said to the cowboy, to the air, to whoever would listen. "Finish up Pedro. We've got to get back on the road." He stood, fumbled in his pocket, and paid the cowboy. Diego nudged his burlap sack, his mother's savings safe.

"We're buddies now, right?" Ralph Preston pressed.

Diego folded his hands in front of his crotch and nodded. Out in the street, his legs felt uncertain, foreign. *I am still in Texas*, he thought, taking some comfort from the rich surroundings, not like his home with its sagging roof and missing porch rails. Ralph Preston talked on and on as they climbed into the truck as if afraid he might run out of words. Diego half-listened, dozy in the hot cab with his full belly.

"Don't get barbecue like that in the big house."

Diego squirmed in his seat. He clutched his sack close. Ralph Preston stared at him. Diego had heard of the big house, a place where Mexicans went and didn't return as Ralph Preston revved the engine and eased the truck forward.

"Why don't you come with me to Dallas? I like company. Makes the road go easy. You can sleep in the truck. I'll be back through Odessa tomorrow and take you on to El Paso. You can show off your sister to me then."

"I have to meet my Papa. He looks for me," Diego said opening the door although the truck crept forward.

"Pedro. Come on. You have a full belly. What is it? The big house? I was just kidding," but Diego was already climbing down the side of the speeding truck. Rocks ricocheted from underneath the tires as the truck gained speed.

Ralph Preston shouted to Diego, "Jump you sorry tamale!"

Chapter 2:
A Woman and a Dog

He heard the slur above all else, above the roar of the big rig's engine as it sped away, above the loud ripping of his pocket where he secreted his Diamond Tips. The barbeque burned in his gut. Diego suffered the indignity of torn pants and bruised knees stolidly. He searched in the brush for his missing shoe and found it dusty and scraped but unharmed. He slipped his foot into the shoe. "One size too big is next year's blessing," his mother often said when he complained about them. He was glad to have them. He had jumped off near the outskirts of Odessa, and Diego heeded his own small wisdom, crossed the highway and headed back to town to look for some shade. It was enough for one day. He would try for a ride later. He would find an unprepossessing alley and sleep for the night. Tomorrow he would go north away from this heat. He thought of his mother and the anger his step-father would show her when they found him missing.

Before he walked a hundred paces, a small, dusty, green station wagon slowed next to him. A woman sat at the wheel, and a dog pressed against the window, his pink tongue lolling. Diego didn't look up, and the woman pulled ahead and stopped the car. As she climbed out of the car, bracing her legs and holding the window handle, Diego could see that she was old.

"Hey, you? Son? You want a ride?" she said as Diego came closer. She still had not made it out of the car, and her fingers gripped a tattered rope that kept the dog from leaping out. "It's mighty hot. Jump in. I'm going to town. That's as far as I ever go." She picked up her legs and pulled them back into the car. The dog started to bark. "She likes you. Come on."

Diego stood at the passenger window and drew swirls on the dusty window. "I'm only going so far." And he pointed to Odessa."

"Then get in. Like I said, that's as far as I'm going."

The woman released the dog's tether as far as Diego's hand. "Her name's Camilla. Don't bite, but she gives you a good licking," and she began to laugh at herself, a thin merry laugh, and Diego got in. Thin, leathery flaps hung on either side of her face where her face had melted, and long, dark pockets kept their own treasures beneath her eyes. Her hair was grey and frosted with white silvery wisps.

"You hold her," and she handed Diego the rope and the small plump dog.

It was a hobo dog. Diego had seen these dogs in El Paso, belonging to no one, warily asking for scraps, but this dog was clean and well-fed. Diego began to relax.

"I pick up children, always have. Not old men, by God, not them. No, I leave them in the dust. I pick up the retarded. You ain't retarded are you?"

"No."

"Didn't think so, but I do pick up Tom Jenkins. Slow, you know, but has a glimmer. I do pick him up. He's from around town. See, I know him in a way. Just put that dog on your lap. He slobbers if he's at the window too long. Like a baby he is. He don't bite, just wants the closeness. Let him on up. He won't settle 'til you do."

Diego didn't want to fuss with the dog, didn't like his face being smothered in drool. He tugged at the rope, but the dog leaped at him. He thought to himself, *Do these English never stop talking?* He was in his own land. They were the interlopers, and he struggled with his words to make the woman stop with no success. He wanted to rest and still shook with the thoughts of Ralph Preston, the jump, his torn pants. Finally, he placed his hand around the dog's neck and slowly pushed him into his lap.

Then as if to herself, she said, "I see something in the retarded, like Camilla here. Won't hurt a body. Might lick them to death though," and she laughed again like a tiny, church bell. "I see something in you." Diego looked straight at the road ahead. They had entered Odessa. "The way you hold your shoulders straight, how you lean into the hitchhike. How your lips were set when I first seen your face. There's more than meets the eye. Where you headed?"

"Odessa."

"I can drive you up to your door. Just tell me where."

"No. Thanks." Diego pressed his fingers into the dog's thick brown fur. Before he had thought it through, before he could shape some false words in his mind, he said, "I'm looking for my Papa."

"Oh well, that's harder. He's lost, ain't he?"

"*Sí*," and Diego put his hand to his face and took in the warm earthy dog.

"Some folks stay lost, you know?"

"*Sí.*"

"Some folks get found. Just depends how you look."

"Here is good," Diego said, pointing to a turquoise bodega.

"You see, she's settled. Likes you I know she does. She's a real detective when it comes to folks. Sees your soul. It ain't tainted yet. Hold onto your soul, son." Diego stroked the dog with one hand, and with the other, his nail scraped against the sulfur of his Diamond Tips hidden in his good pocket.

She slowed the car and pulled into the curb. "I'll pick you up on the way back from where you're going. Always do. If I see you on the other side of the road, you've got a ride. They always come back. I hear some sorry tales. I see them coming out of the city and back again. Perhaps they'll be an oil man. Maybe a movie star. Could happen. But they come back. Across the city and back like they been damned up. I pick them up whatever."

Diego squirmed, restless to leave, but he could not let go of the rope. He could not leave the dog. He could steal the dog. She would never be able to chase him, but he was not tainted yet. That's what she'd said. He let go the rope and opened the door. He stood at the window to say goodbye and thank you.

"You won't find ordinary folk to give you a ride. Keep your wits about you." And before Diego could mouth the words goodbye, she was speeding down the road kicking up a fine yellow dust.

Chapter 3:
The Salesman from Baltimore

Diego was still smarting from the kick in the dust. *"Cerdo,"* he muttered. Ralph Preston had looked like a pig, ate like a pig. Diego remembered hotly the red drool that crept across his chin, the tongue slathering around his mouth, the stench of pig eating pig. Diego would never eat barbecue again. He walked in the hot sun to the bodega. It was a small, square building, the turquoise paint glinting off the walls. He squinted as he entered the dark store. Tiny bells jangled. He was met with a cool rush of air. A fan hummed on the counter. He clutched his burlap bag as a man came out from a door in the back. He looked Diego over from top to bottom.

"*Como está?*" he said, stroking his fat cheek. "*Qué quiere?*"

Diego didn't need help. He had quickly looked the store over. "*Nada, gracias.*" He walked slowly down the aisle while the man followed some distance behind. Diego wanted a cool drink. He had the money and jangled his sack to show his good faith to the man. Again and again, the coins jingled, and the man retreated to help a customer who had entered the store. Diego found the cans of beans, red and green and tempting. He looked around, his eyes darting left and right, and gently stuck two of the cans into his bag. The coins jingled. The man's voice rose as he found some tomatoes for the customer. A big box stood next to the door. It held a rainbow of drinks in clear glass bottles. Diego lifted the lid. Mist rose up out of the box.

"*Veinte céntavos,*" the man shouted across the store. Diego felt the man's small, black eyes boring into the back of his head. He pulled out a frosty, orange bottle, held it up, and made as if to drink, his sack slung over his other shoulder. The man smiled broadly. Diego made his way to the counter. He placed the drink on the counter and smiled brokenly back, lowering his sack to the floor. He knew coins, dimes, thin and slippery, nickels, broad and flat, pennies, copper and poor. He stooped, stuck his hand into the sack, and pulled out two thin dimes, knowing their worth just by feel. He slapped them gently before the man's hands that lay flat on the counter and noticed the man's apron, bloodied with meat. Saliva moistened Diego's parched mouth. The man scooped the coins up, while the other customer edged toward the counter his hands full of tomatoes. They began talking, friends perhaps, and the man motioned toward the big box, held up the orange drink and mimed opening the bottle, while he continued talking. A bottle opener was fastened to the side of the box with a string. Diego could use this opener. He tugged at the string that held the opener fast. It gave, and he quickly his it in his cupped palm. He was glad that he was thinking about everything. He opened his drink before leaving the store, and gulped a mouthful of sweet orange soda. Diego smiled at the man at the back of the store, and the man smiled back and waved, the bells jingling behind Diego as he struck out into the searing sun.

By late afternoon, Diego knew he had to find a place to sleep before dark. The woman and her dog had dropped him in one of the Mexican neighborhoods which were famous for their alleys. He would find an alley and rest. He skirted the main road, looking for a quiet avenue, houses huddled close, laundry on the line, flowers in broken bottles, and rusted cans. He savored the drink, drinking slowly, saving some for later. He passed a group of young boys playing mumbly peg. They looked up as Diego passed, but their attention was fixed on the game, the thrown knife standing straight and shiny. As he had expected, the homes were riddled with alleyways. Looking behind, he ducked into a narrow lane between two houses. It was full of everything Diego needed. He tore a shirt and pants from a line in a backyard and stuffed it into his sack. He found a shed behind a small adobe home. He felt a moment of homesickness but washed it away with his orange drink. People would be eating, he thought, and he untied the rope that held the door fast. He slid inside. It was dark and cool and dusty with dried chicken shit. Baskets of garlic hung from the rafter. It was small and full. Sacks of grain stood in one corner. He opened one and poured it into the stolen shirt and tied it so the grain would not spill. Diego stuck a dented pot into his bag. He sat and leaned against a mud-encrusted wheelbarrow and went over his treasures.

He had not thought of these things when he had crept out of his stepfather's cabin. *Going*, he had thought, *going. Nothing else except the Diamond Tips*. He took the red and blue box out of his pocket. He shook the box, loved the sound of the little wooden sticks. He would light one, he thought, then thought better of it. Later. He stuck the box back into his pocket and grasped the thin scraps of paper he had salvaged from the road. Little light swept into the shed, but Diego pored over them anyway, whispering the words he could make out aloud. Traffic accident on Route 10, 3 cups of sugar, oil found in gulch.

When the light ebbed, a chicken-scratched its way from the back of the shed, and Diego worried someone would come to feed them. Then another and another. He would have to leave early before he was found. The chickens clucked fearfully as if a rattlesnake were present, disliking their nest disturbed, scratching the dirt floor. Diego settled into a corner behind the wheelbarrow. He grasped a can of beans from his sack, stood his orange drink within reach and dug the opener from his pocket. *These things*, he thought, *made him strong, not just a runaway boy.* He bent the opener over the can and made cuts all around the metal top. The chickens scrabbled around him, and Diego kicked his foot out in the dark. He ate with his fingers, scooping up large mouthfuls. He thought of his mother's rice and beans. When the can was empty, he put it into his sack. He finished the last of the orange drink, put the cap on, and stored it away with his treasures. He would need water sometime. He was pleased with his thoughts. He was scared of the dark, the chickens' murmur, but he fell asleep anyway. It was the light he liked.

He woke in the night to a thick, black darkness. He had startled a chicken, which had roosted against his leg, and its squawks frightened him. He cooed and reached for the bird, but she scuttled away, still scolding. He knew if she had been in reach he would have strangled the hen. He scrabbled in his burlap sack for the Diamond Tips and the scraps of paper he had scavenged from the road. The match skittered across the rough surface, and the shed was eerily lit. He fed the paper to the flame on the wheelbarrow's bed, and he felt his heart calming. The chickens all awoke at once, and one darted out of the hole in the shed. As the paper faded and curled, its edges frayed with orange embers, he gave a deep breath. The last words that became blackened read 'homeward.' As the shed was suddenly swept to black again, he sounded out the word.

His father, not the man with the harsh voice who lived in their house, but the man who built things, barns, houses, coffins, the man who left Sunday after church in the heart of summer careened into his mind. Diego's fascination with fire had sprung from this man's loins. His father was fire itself, dancing, darting, quick to anger, subsiding slow and lazy like a dying fire.

Often his father was called upon to tear buildings down, a roofless barn, the rotting timbers of a house. His father hated this work. He would prefer to watch structures rise. He would stand on the roof of destructive labor and howl to the sun. Like Diego, he was afraid of the night.

The week before he left he stood on the lawn with his claw hammer taking nails from rotted timbers. When he had collected every last nail, he built a fire with coal. It was hotter than a brush fire, meant to burn the devil from his hiding place. He scattered the nails into the fire while Diego watched.

"*Qué son eso?*" Diego asked, wanting to be near the fire, his father.

"*Clavos del ataúd,*" his father spat. Coffin nails.

Diego knew they were for coffins. His father would not waste anything. He straightened these nails for death. He dared not risk the anger his father would have for him, but he wanted to know who had died. Had he missed something?

"*Quién morió?*"

His father would not look at him and instead pounded the nails straight. He remained silent until all the nails stood in a row, and he was ready to nail a coffin shut. Though Diego wanted to run, he stood there silently. His father stuck the hammer into the fire and then flung it at the burning sky.

"*Quizás sea yo*, maybe it's me," he shouted and ran off to strip another board from the rotting house.

Diego, only five, knew about death. His grandfather had died, and shortly thereafter, his grandmother had passed away. His father had built their coffins, had used the straightened nails to close their lids. But his father dead? That was ridiculous, and Diego risked a laugh. As his father strode across the clearing, a board across his chest, the spitting image of the Christ in church, Diego ran.

He kept quiet that day and for several days after, not bothering his father with questions. He had stored so many things to ask that he felt burdened, and when he finally went to find his father to ask him, he was gone as if in a puff of smoke. He was sure his father had died. He had said as much, hadn't he? "Maybe it's me," he had said. But when he searched the other laborers' cabins on the ranch, he found a coffin had not been prepared. He had seen burials. The dead were buried in the field above the river. "A good view," the Boss had said at his grandfather's funeral. He searched the burying grounds for freshly dug earth, but there was nothing, not even a shovelful of upturned earth.

Diego asked his mother what had happened to his father. She grew red and said she could not be bothered, but Diego hung onto her skirt until she finally whispered, "The devil has taken him away." Diego asked where, but his mother said she could not say. She did not know.

Diego refused to cry. Instead, he gathered scraps of paper from the trash heap and stored them away in a burlap sack. The next time he carried eggs to the Boss' kitchen, he stole the box of Diamond Tips from the kitchen hearth. He would go away from the ranch then, for hours, and strike the matches onto the paper, willing his father to return.

Diego woke before dawn. He scuttled into the stolen clothes, ill-fitting but clean. He balled his clothes with the chicken stench and threw them into a corner. Though he tried to hush them, the remaining chickens skittered about and finally fled out the hole in the shed wall. The dry, dusty chicken manure had given him a great thirst, but the orange soda was gone, and he feared going back to the bodega. Stealthily he opened the shed door, looked around and began to thread his way through the intricate alleys as if he had mapped them. He passed a wandering hobo dog, brown and stubby, who sniffed the air. Diego pulled down his pants and pissed in the dog's direction marking the territory as his. When he was back out on the street, lone trucks, their headlights blazing, rode warily through the streets as if they too were not quite awake. His stomach growled, and he thought of the other can of beans in his sack. Though he wanted to pry them from the can, he resisted, thinking to save them for a crisis.

The smells of morning hit him like a brick, biscuits baking, coffee boiling in tin pans, eggs frying. He walked down the street to the bodega. It was not yet open. He stood on the sidewalk where the woman with the dog had let him off. For the first time since he had run, Diego felt lost.

It was too sudden, barely dawn when the car swerved onto the road beside Diego. He had barely faced the meager traffic. He had only waved at the oncoming car.

"Sam Baschom," the driver boomed from the open window, "Salesman from Baltimore!" He took his hands from the steering wheel and spread his arms wide to take in the myriad boxes that crammed his station wagon. His voice was loud, crisp, silky, and smooth, something Diego remembered from his mother's lullabies. The man wore a suit, grey, striped, crumpled. His tie was loosened around his neck. He was sweating.

"Ball Bearings!" he added.

Diego did not know bearings, and it struck him that the boxes might be full of miniature balls. His curiosity piqued, he walked to the passenger window. He held up his burlap sack shoulder high as if it were a flag, ready to say no when the man spoke.

"Going to Sweetwater. Going to hole up for the day. I've been driving all night. Then on to Dallas. You want a ride? I could use the company to keep me awake."

It occurred to Diego then that he go could back. Two or three rides. Maybe it was enough, and he could go back to the ranch. Maybe it hadn't all gone so badly. Maybe they would welcome him with open arms and simple worry.

"Sweetwater it is. You coming or what?" Diego sensed a resigned anger in the man's voice.

Diego stirred, his feet shifting in the gravel. Maybe it had not gone as he hoped. "*Sí, gracias,*" Diego said and reached for the door's handle.

"Back seat is all I can offer. Here give me your bag."

"No. I hold it," he said clutching the bag to his chest.

"Suit yourself."

Diego wedged himself into the narrow space that was not littered with small cardboard boxes. The seat in front was piled high with papers that fluttered as Sam Baschom drove forward.

"So much paper," Diego said as he squirmed in his seat. "You read all these?"

"Most everything. This car is my office you could say. I travel. These are the pay stubs," and he laughed like quicksilver. "Inventory sheets, sales slips, letters from the boss. General delivery, of course, depending where I am."

Diego knew boss. He knew he could not steal these even if he wanted to.

"You read?"

"Some. I read some," Diego hesitated.

"Good. Read this out to me while I drive. It's my next stop." Sam Baschom reached into the pile of papers, one hand on the wheel, and clutched a handful of letters and handed them back to Diego.

Diego's hand trembled as he clutched the creamy thick papers. "Sweetwater El-ectrate."

"Electric. You doing good boy. Down on the left should be a list of the ball bearing sizes they'll need. It's just letters and numbers but means a heck of a lot to me. Don't want to show up empty-handed. Just read them off."

Diego read the letters and numbers. He could do this. He felt pride in his own voice as if the man had hired him on as if he were part of a bigger machine until he saw that his fingers had left dirty prints on the paper. He dropped the papers into his lap.

"What is it?" Sam Baschom asked.

"Just one more," and he read it off slowly straining to see the letters and numbers where they sat on his lap.

"Good. I think I have everything. Thanks. You'll make a good assistant someday," and he reached back for the papers. Diego passed the papers to the man face down hoping the salesman would not see the dirty impressions his fingers had left. But Sam Baschom didn't. He seemed to move on like the car, like Diego, from one place to another.

"You hungry?"

"I am. *Sí.*"

28

Sam Baschom pulled a brown paper sack from beneath his legs and handed it to Diego.

"Doughnuts."

Diego had heard of doughnuts but had not ever had sweet breads except for the rolls his mother made for Christmas breakfast. He pulled a round sugary doughnut from the bag and started to hand it back to Sam Baschom.

"No, keep it. I eat too many," and he patted his firm round belly.

Diego couldn't believe his luck. As he bit into the sugary mound, another sweetness of jelly reached his tongue. He wondered if the trip were long, if, indeed, he might become Sam Baschom's assistant. The space he was sitting in no longer felt so confining. The boxes in the seats and in the rear of the car suddenly seemed full of gold. He ate three doughnuts each one unlike the other. The remaining two he thought to stick in his sack, but thinking Sam Baschom would think him greedy, he placed the brown paper sack on the ball bearing boxes where Sam Baschom could see them in his rearview mirror.

"What's your name?" Sam Baschom called.

His voice was innocent and friendly, and Diego hesitated before lying again. "Pedro Gómez."

"Where are you headed?"

"Sweetwater."

"Visiting family, a waiting job, or a sweetheart?" he winked into the rearview mirror. "They say sweethearts are sweeter in Sweetwater."

Diego didn't want to lie to Sam Baschom. Though it went against his grain, Diego said, "My father. I'm looking for my Papa."

"He's in Sweetwater?"

"He could be. He could be anywhere. I try Sweetwater."

"Why Sweetwater?"

The water there was sweeter than anywhere else in the world. His Papa had told him. He had a picture of his father kneeling by the water, anointing himself, perhaps holy water, last rites, perhaps only thirsty. He knew he would not become Sam Baschom's assistant. He knew he would not read numbers and letters. He knew he would not delight in doughnuts or share in Sam Baschom's friendly wink. He knew the ride would end, so he started to lie.

"My Papa is a singer. Sweet like a bird," Diego lied. Manuel, his father, though he could build fine things, could not sing a note. Diego fluttered his hands over the front seat. "Like bird."

"Is he away singing now? Is that why you're going to Sweetwater?"

"Like bird he is. Not only singing but traveling. Place to place they want him. Money is good. Maybe in Sweetwater he play. I have not heard. He travels much. I am looking."

"Do you sing?"

"I sing too, but not like Papa. Not sweet and remembering."

"Sing me something."

Diego, in spite of his lies, sang well. Not like a bird exactly, but music soft and hidden. He hummed the lullabies his mother sang to fend off the night.

"I like it. Sounds like morning ghosts."

"A lullaby my Mama sings to me."

Diego sang all of the lullabies his mother had ever sung, and then more, songs that pulsed from the earth, from the light, and Diego smiled at the songs that sprang from nowhere and everywhere.

Sam Baschom's fingers tapped lightly on the steering wheel. Diego stopped singing to eat another doughnut offering the last one to Sam Baschom. He took it, his arm arched over backwards, sugar spilling onto the seat and the precious cardboard boxes. As they ate in silence, the gentle lullabies hovering around them, Diego believed in his lies.

Pedro is good name, he thought. *His Papa a famous singer, and he, too, born into the tradition.* His lies lifted him, and he didn't feel the cardboard boxes or hear their contents rattling. When the lullabies were spent, had drifted out of reach, he smelled the empty brown paper bag. The salesman had talked like running water, football, baseball, the great wide Texas sky, how you could feel lost in it. He talked so long Diego lost the thread of his words and fell into sleep. He dozed for a time dreaming in darkness when he woke with a start. The car sat beside the road idling.

"Thought you'd never wake up."

"Where?" Diego asked bewildered, still half asleep.

"You were supposed to keep me awake. Almost rode off the road back there," and the salesman pointed into the distance behind him.

"Sorry."

"It's okay. I guess the lullabies got to you?"

"*Sí.*"

"Pretty."

"*Sí.*"

Sam Baschom sat behind the wheel, the engine idling. Pedro clutched the brown paper bag.

"I'll let you off here," Sam Baschom said, looking into the rearview mirror, behind Diego as if he were counting the blades of buffalo grass that grew alongside the road. "Midland's just ahead. A mile or so."

"You said Sweetwater."

"I said I'd give you a ride. Have a stop to make first." He winked at Diego in the rearview mirror.

Diego picked up a box of ball bearings and shook it. The air clanked and rattled, charged.

"I have work to do," the impatience welling beneath his sugary words. "They frown on us picking up riders. Anyone could spot me. I'm known around here. It's my territory."

Papers fluttered with the hot, sudden breeze. It was then Diego reached for the Diamond Tips in his pocket. *If he wanted, Sam Baschom could make him an assistant,* he thought. He could carry the boxes. He could in a stroke pick out the small from the large. Sam Baschom drummed to the cadence of one of Diego's lullabies, his fingers striking the steering wheel, gently, slowly.

"It's been swell having you along for the ride. I would have slept myself into the grass or another car without your singing. I hope you find your father."

The papers fluttered again, and still, Diego sat in the corner of the car. Diego had pulled a matchstick from the box, was rubbing the tip against his thumb. He could light the paper bag, the bag that had promised everything. He could drop a lit match onto the papers in the front seat. It would catch, light, and flare. He struck the match against his fingernail. It lit. The papers fluttered. He could leave this man with the wide grin, his promise of a future.

Sam Baschom turned then, looked into Diego's black eyes.

"I've got to go, son."

Diego licked his fingertips and squelched the lit match.

"I'm thinking on it. Was all," he said tucking the spent match into his pocket.

"I know," the salesman said, revving the engine.

In one quick motion, Diego reached for the handle, opened the door, and stood outside. The ball bearings clanked in chorus as Sam Baschom sped off.

Chapter 4:
Millie

As soon as Sam Baschom's tires hit the asphalt, a battered brown four-door swerved onto the brush behind Diego. The driver honked her horn over and over again, and Diego stepped back as she edged the car ever closer. The afternoon light prevented Diego from seeing the driver, and he began walking toward Midland.

"Git back here!" a woman shouted. Diego pretended he hadn't heard. "You heard me young man. Git back here!" Wisps of metallic grey hair softened the otherwise stern face. She was half in and half out of the car, a plump, blousy woman. "Don't make me take after you!"

Diego turned then.

"Git in!" she shouted again. "Git in this car this minute." Diego didn't know whether he should run or stand.

"I go to Sweetwater," he finally stuttered.

She shook her head. "What could your parents be thinking? Git in this car this minute. Was that your last ride?" she asked, pointing down the highway.

"*Sí*," and since Diego could not think what else to say to her fury, he sputtered. "Sam Baschom."

"Of course. Sam Baschom. It could just have easily been Fred Astaire, and you wouldn't know the difference." She shook her head again. "I'm only going to say it one more time. Git in. You don't want to see an old woman chasing you down the brush, now do you?"

"No."

"Good now we're getting somewhere. I'm Millicent Towney. You can call me Millie. Everybody else does. Look at it this way. I'm your patron saint. Get in. I don't bite much."

Before Diego succumbed, he asked, grasping his bag, "Which?"

"Which what," she said, grasping the car door, unsteady.

Which *santo*?

"Which saint? How should I know? I'm Baptist, Southern. How about Spencer Tracy, the patron saint of wayward boys? What are you all of thirteen? You shouldn't be takin' rides with strangers."

"Which one," Diego repeated, feeling a firestorm well up, his hand dug deep in his pocket for the matchsticks.

"Saint Francis weren't it? The patron saint of animals, maybe children. It don't matter. Git in. I'm meltin'." She came around the car and opened the door.

As Diego stood there standing away from the sun, his back to her, her words railing, Diego remembered a time when he had provoked one of the Boss' ranch dogs. It was a grisly thing, tufts of fur missing, a thin knobby tail, and it leaped for the stick he held and had bitten him. He swung with his other arm and battered the dog's head until it let go, its ear bleeding. His mother had punished him. His mother had evoked Saint Francis to heal the dog. He, too, like Diego, had been an ordinary boy doing bad things, bad works against God and man. She said he had even gone to prison and then he found Jesus. She promised him that prison would not happen to Diego. You are a good boy," she had said, "but Saint Francis who looks after everything in nature would be disappointed."

Diego had been shamed. His punishment was to wash the crusted saddle blankets. He had fetched the boiling water, the dirty blankets that smelled of sweat and horses and rides, who knew where, then scrubbing with a long, wooden paddle, then hanging them to dry. The other ranch boys watched and hollered but from a safe distance, wary of Diego's anger.

Millie, impatient with Diego's rudeness said, "I have a farm. I'll take you there, feed and clean you up. Git in now. My rheumatiz is acting up."

Diego turned then, knowing she was not a patron saint, but perhaps his messenger and strode stiffly to the car. When they were seated, she cried. "Phewie! You been in a cockfight?"

Diego knew cockfight. The men on the ranch circled around a bevy of roosters. Their claws razor sharp, the birds clawed, leaped, and struck at one another until paper money passed from hand to hand. Some of the birds died, their beautiful flamelike feathers limp and gone. His father was not permitted to play. It was for the white men only, their beefy arms, drool spilling down their mouths as they watched and rooted for their favorite. His father waited for a carcass that never came.

"*Sí.* I play the birds."

"You ever won?"

"*Sí.* Many times. We get plenty birds. Some fight."

"I'm goin' to take you home. We'll get you cleaned up some and fed, and then I'll take you where you wanna go."

They drove right up to the beginnings of Midland in silence, then Millie veered off on a straight track of road, that finally curved and bent south of the city. Farms dotted the landscape like forgotten stars, some closed and boarded, others bright open beacons. It was to one of the ghost farms that Millie drove. The drive was a quarter mile or so, and Diego sat uneasily at Millie's side, the land spreading out to the blazing horizon, the farmhouse white and lonely.

"It ain't much, is it?"

"No, not much."

"It's all Rupert left. He died in the front room," she said slowing and then parking the car.

Diego stepped out onto the brown, dried earth. The grasses had withered and formed small dusty clumps. The swayback porch reminded Diego of home, and it creaked under his feet.

Millie opened the door.

"I don't lock up. Nothing to steal even if I did." Diego hung back. "Come on. You can't go around smellin' like a dung heap. Git on in there."

Diego stepped gingerly into a wide hallway. It smelled of empty closed up air, abandoned air, a vacant expanse. Diego smelled himself, and he cursed the chickens.

"Is big?"

"Yeh, it's big all right. Closed up the half of it. Don't have no use for five bedrooms. Jes keep the front room, kitchen and the bath, a bedroom or two of course. You'll find the bath next to the kitchen, in there," and she pointed down the hallway. "Strip yourself, and I'll find you some clean clothes and stir up some grub."

Diego hesitated. He would have felt surer if he had the clean clothes in his hand.

"Pants?"

"I've raised five children. I guess I've seen a million bottoms. But if you're bashful I'll find you Rupert's work pants. Stay here. Don't want you stinkin' up the rest of the house." She disappeared through the front room, and Diego could hear her slowly and painfully climb some stairs.

When she returned, she held blue denim pants, a red checkered shirt, and underwear. "Here," she said, handing him the parcel. "In here now," she said, leading him down the once yellow, flowered, wallpapered hall. "The hot's on the left. Let it run a bit before you get in, or you'll end up a scalded pig," and she went on down the hall to the kitchen.

Cautiously Diego opened the door. A washstand and tub dominated the small bath. He peeled off the stolen shirts and pants and stood naked before the washstand mirror. Bug and spider bites swelled red and festering along his chest. His cheeks were still smudged with donut sugar. He wondered where Sam Baschom was now. His stomach growled. He was startled with a sharp knock on the door, and he clutched his dirty clothes to his privates.

"You gonna take all day. Get a move on. I've got a griddle just fixed for pancakes and sausage. Don't dilly dally," and she knocked again.

Diego turned the hot water handle.

"Better," she said, and Diego heard her walk away.

Diego put his hand under the running water. It was cool but threaded with a warm rising. He waited for some minutes until his hand burned under the faucet and then set the cold to running. Slowly, the waters mixed, and Diego stood in wonder. He set the plug and watched the rising water. He looked around for soap and a cloth, dunked his toe, and satisfied, lowered himself into the tub. When the tub was half full and meeting his belly, Diego scrunched down under the water until his hair was soaked. He worked top downward, scrubbing his hair, his chest, his arms, belly, and privates. He leaned over and scrubbed his legs. The water smelled putrid, a mixture of dust and manure. The clear water had turned brown. Diego pulled the plug, then set the water to running again. When it was full, he rinsed his head and body and climbed out of the tub. He reached for the towel and rubbed himself dry. The clothes were too big, those of a man, not a boy, but Diego put them on anyway, holding up the pants with his hands. He wanted to leave it as he had found it, and he replaced the soap in its dish, wiping the tub with the towel and hanging it up to dry. When he was satisfied, he walked into the hallway and made his way to the kitchen. He could smell things cooking.

Millie eyed him from head to toe.

"Much better. Come here though I'm gonna smell you down. If you still smell of chicken, it's back you go." Diego obeyed and stood before her. "Now that smells like a clean boy. Have a seat over there."

Diego began to sit when she cried.

"Not there. There. That's Rupert's seat."

"*Perdoname,*" Diego said quickly rising and took a seat away from her.

Diego was pleased with this seat. He could see the door out of the house, the long kitchen counter where she stood with her back to him cooking. He could smell the sausage and a faint wisp of soap that lingered. A plate, stacked high with sausage and a platter where she scooped pancakes, sat beside her. When she turned toward him, the platter of pancakes in hand, she smiled, a faint hope flickered across her face, and something in Diego's countenance softened toward her. He rose to help her.

"Why you must be hungry to be such a gentleman," and she handed the platter to him and returned with the sausage. She placed a pitcher of milk beside him and retrieved a glass pitcher of water.

"You take your pick, though it's said you can get drunk on water. Rupert's proof. Would down water all day long, pitcher after pitcher, and become as silly as a parrot before noon."

"I like milk."

"Drink all you want then."

Diego poured milk and waited for Millie to serve herself.

"There's no standin' on ceremony here. Help yourself."

With the concentration worthy of an engineer, Diego stacked his pancakes high layering each pancake with soft melted butter then slathering the whole with warmed syrup. He placed the sausages neatly around the pancakes. When he looked up, Mille was crying.

"Why?"

"I'm a silly old fool. Rupert dressed his pancakes and sausage in just the same way," she said wiping her face with her napkin. "Eat, 'fore it gets cold."

She ate sparingly, watching Diego. Finally, she spoke.

"Lawd, I've had a boy naked in my bath, and I don't even know his name."

"Diego," he said. "Diego Ramírez." Something caught in his throat as he spoke truthfully.

"Mexican?"

Diego thought carefully of his answers, thinking of the hundreds of chores he would have to do to give thanks.

"*Sí.*"

A clock ticked somewhere in the distance, and Diego thought of his mother knitting baby clothes for the church. His pants almost fit with his now distended belly. Diego watched Millie as she picked away at her pancakes. A smoky grey cat curled against his calves, and he reached down to pet him.

"Don't feed him. He's my rat catcher. A good one too. Don't want him to get used to scraps. I leave a pan of water for him on the porch. You'd think that being nothin' here, there wouldn't be no rats, but you'd be surprised," and she stood and took her plate away to the sink. Diego rose too and carried the platters and plates, cups and glasses, forks and knives to the counter. Millie ran the water, swishing her hand under the current, pouring in soap and began to wash the dishes. Diego grabbed a clean, dry towel and dried them, and they worked together in quiet efficiency. The cat, sitting in the center of the kitchen, stood guard. When everything was clean, the cat scurried out the screen door.

When they were done, Millie said, "You'll need a bit of rope for them pants. Come with me." She led him out the screen door onto the porch and searched in a wooden bucket until she found some laundry rope. With some pruning shears, she cut a length of rope. "Tie this through the loops. The pants will fit better. No. No. Even in Rupert's clothes, you don't look a bit like him."

Diego followed her back inside, and she led him into a sitting room at the front of the house.

"Rupert would sit here for hours. He worked hard, and I never minded. Ran a cattle farm. Not big, but not little either," she said, waving toward Rupert's chair. "He'd butcher them himself, a bloody business if you ask me, and sell the meat in town. Midland was a boom town then. Oil everywhere. Lot of farmers sold out. Not Rupert. He'd truck what he could into Sweetwater. Folks loved his beef. Then years of drought brought him down. Couldn't afford the feed then couldn't afford the cattle. His last year, he raised nothin'. Oil boomed. Died of a broken heart, you ask me. Standin' one day, bedridden the next. Used to sit right here," and she pointed to the tattered brown armchair. "Sat there until he died one day. I sit there mornings and afternoons if I have the notion and sometimes I hear him rattling around the house."

Diego knew ghosts. They haunted his dreams, flying at him in an unearthly white light.

He could not make out their eyes, but their mouths would contort, and he could see the fissures on their lips, the words beyond his hearing. He would wake sweating, crying with their unspoken words in his mouth. "I'll walk to town," Diego muttered.

"You'll do no such thing. You'll spend the night. In the morning I'll take you," and she sat in Rupert's chair and the hair rose on the back of Diego's neck.

"He's long gone, Diego. Though not a church-going man, he had his beliefs. He believed in the land. That was enough. You may hear him in the rocker on the porch. But he's not up to any mischief. Now go. Poke around. See if there's anything useful in the barn. I'm gonna nap some."

When Diego walked to the barn, he thought, *perhaps there's something useful here, something to take, maybe even a keepsake.* The barn was perfect for a fire with its mounds of dry, scattered straw, broken timbers, a cracked wooden wagon, cobwebs stretched to eternity. Her kindness, her familiarity had stung. *Who was she to take him in, dress him the ghost man's clothes?* Even now his tongue recoiled from the lingering taste of syrup. *Sweetness in overalls,* he thought and spat. She knew only his name which she had probably forgotten while she drifted in sleep. He could set this fire without harm, and his heart quickened, and his hands trembled. The barn was a fair distance from the house, all but abandoned, the breeze southerly. She would sleep in peace. He would set the fire and be done with it. After the thump of rafters blazing, he would walk into town.

He would chant his angel prayer as he did at every fire before he took out his Diamond Tips.

"O my dear Angel Guardian, preserve me from the misfortune of offending God."

The chant conjured up his stepfather's croaking laughter, the laugh that came readily to him after he had striped Diego's naked flanks. The welts he would have to hide from his mother with the threat of more if he did not stifle his tears and cries. He had been seven. His stepfather had been in the house for two months.

As if this secrecy was some sort of sweet pact between them, he'd say with his crooked smile, "My Dolly. Don't go to your Mama," his arm sweeping the room, his belt slapping his thigh. Looping the belt, his leather weapon, into his pant stays, he would grin again, slamming the door as he went out to supper.

Diego would dress slowly, dabbing at blood secreted from his mother, and take his place at the table answering his Mama's questions about the ranch, about the coyotes, about rattlesnakes, of which she was fearful.

Diego gathered a small mound of straw. He shivered though the barn was hot, sweltering. He would set this fire and be done with it. Millie's husband trickled into his thoughts, how like him Diego was, but Diego knew he would not grow up to own a farm and see it go under. He knew he was unlike this man. He took out his Diamond Tips. He settled cross-legged on the floor before the straw and made the sign of the cross.

He closed his eyes, the faces racing toward him as they always did, eyes drooping, their faces melted by fire, the hands gripped and charred. His mother and sisters' faces fled, but his stepfather's face eluded him. He chanted his Angel Guardian prayer again hoping to conjure the bastard when a shout startled him from his plans. He quickly scattered the straw, hid his matches and stood.

Millie stood at the doorway.

"Didn't find anything useful? I didn't expect it, but Rupert could be cagey, hiding things within things. Come on in. I've fixed us some lunch."

Diego swept the porch before Millie descended upon him with a tray of sweet pickles, jelly sandwiches, and glasses of milk.

"Sit in Rupert's rocker. He'd be glad it was making some use."

"Where's he buried?"

"On the land, of course!" Millie said, slapping her thighs. "I'll show you if you want. It's out beyond the vegetable garden. Gives a good view of the property. But landsakes," she said and turned to Diego, "a boy like you hasn't need of ghosts."

Diego's face went dark, and they ate silently except for the crunch of pickle.

"Where are you off to tomorrow?" she said wiping her mouth with a napkin.

"Looking."

"Your father?"

"*Sí.*"

"Boys are always looking for their Pa. It's the way of the world."

"He sings."

"If he's a singer like you say, there are a few bars in town that sport singers. I'll take you there."

"*Gracias*, but no. I am going Sweetwater."

"Then I'll take you there. If you don't find your Pa, you can come back with me."

"*Gracias.*"

"No thanks needed. I've boys of my own, all grown. No thanks needed."

Diego found the radio, pulled it from its dusty plug, and brought it outside and placed it on the windowsill. They spent the afternoon playing tic tac toe in the shade of the porch and listening to Tennessee Ernie Ford sing "The Shotgun Boogie."

"Does your Pa sing like that?"

"He sings the songs from home. *Celito Lindo.*"

"I like the old songs too," she said as Diego won another round of tic tac toe.

Everything about her was sugar and salt, the pork ribs she served for supper, the corner of the bed turned down, the scratchy blanket. He slept fitfully, whispered his angel prayer into the pillow. Sugar and salt. He tried to grasp it, but could not. The years had made her crusty but pliable. She had no need and his was great. He almost got up in the middle of the night to set the fire but fell wearily into sleep.

In the morning she made him bathe again. "You don't know where you'll be. You may not have a chance," she said, closing the door on him, her voice throaty.

She gave him another shirt, wrapped up his old clothes in brown paper and twine, which Diego placed in his burlap sack, and told him to keep Rupert's clothes.

"You keep them. He was a bigger man than you're gonna be, but they'll do."

She wrapped up the ribs in tin foil and the morning's leftover biscuits. And they set off for Sweetwater.

They rode over the flat land in the harsh light, mindless of Rupert's ghost rocking in the chair in the distance behind them. The road roared beneath them. By midday they neared Sweetwater. Millie scuffled in her seat, her left hand groping in her sweater. She pulled a crumpled five dollar bill and handed it across to Diego.

"You'll need this," she said, her voice gruff.

Diego noticed the raw, rough hands that held the bill. "I cannot."

"Of course you can," and she dropped the five dollars into his lap. As she pulled into the curb before the Prairie Run Bar, she asked, staring straight ahead, "What's your Mama thinking about all of this?"

Gathering the fallen money and placing it on the seat beside him, he knew he was damned even before the words were out of his mouth. "My Mama's dead," his voice low and steady, picturing his Mama's round body as lifeless as he had said. "No!" he cried.

"You don't have to explain. It's a painful world. I'm sorry I asked. You ain't nothin' but a poor orphan boy searchin' for his Pa," and as Diego looked at her, she met him with eyes full of pity.

"No," he said, trying to right the lie as he stuffed the bill into his sack. "She look after me."

"The mysterious ways of the Lord," she said knowingly. "There just ain't no way of knowing, 'cept she brought you to my door. I can't rightly let you go on."

But Diego was out of the car trying to free his rope belt from the seat.

"I go on. Look for my Papa. Thank you, Miss Millie."

She leaned across the seat and called out the open door, "I'll wait right here. If you don't find him, you come right on back. There's another bar across town's got singing. You got that?"

"*Sí*," and Diego closed the car door.

He knew he had brought about his own kind of death. He looked at Milllie's car. She stared through the dusty glass at him and nodded. Diego waved and walked inside.

The entrance of the bar was a screen door encrusted with the carcasses of numerous insects. The scratched, wooden door hung awry on its hinges. A radio blared country music inside. A dusty upright piano stood in one corner. Diego and his damning words had made all thought of his mother in the past tense. We reap what we sow, his mother's ghost whispered in his ear. He stood on the sill believing he had no right to Millie's kindness.

The room was dark and only streams of sunlight filtered in along the cracks in the closed curtains. Behind a long wooden bar stood bottles of amber, and honey, blackness, and sand. A man, his shirtsleeves rolled up to his elbows, a limp brown cloth slung over one arm, looked up. "We don't serve kids," he shouted over the music.

"I'm looking for my Papa," Diego said weakly, his lies carrying no weight.

"It's morning. The regulars don't come in until the sun goes down," he said, swiping at the bar with the brown cloth. "Who is it you're looking for?"

"Papa."

"You said that already," he snapped, slapping at the bar with his cloth. "What's his name?"

Diego involuntarily responded to the man's anger as if slapped himself, as if his stepfather stood in the man's place. He walked over to where the man polished a whiskey glass.

"Manuel Ramirez," Diego snarled, once more drunk on his lies. "He's a singer."

"Could have heard of him," the man said, turning his back on Diego, replacing the whiskey glass to its place on a pyramid of glasses. "Have had lots of singers go through here."

"He sings like a bird."

"Sure kid. They all do," he said turning around again. "I'll ask about him. My customers, especially the drunks, remember every word sung in here. I'll ask, but you can't stay in here. Don't allow no kids. Respectable."

Diego noticed the scarred tables clustered around a wooden palette.

"They sing there?"

"Yup. Like birds," and he laughed and waved his cloth in the air.

Diego stepped onto the wooden palette next to the piano and began to sing *Ceilito Lindo*. The man snapped off the radio, leaned into the love song against all good common sense, swayed with the movement of Diego's slow, moody rendition. When Diego sang the last line, before he had even sung the final chorus, "*Cielito lindo, que a mi me toca,*" the bartender started clapping.

"You're good, not a bird, but you're good. Get that from your Papa?" he said, giving the bar a large sweep with the cloth.

"*Sí.*"

"They like the Spanish songs here. Maybe you could sing the songs tonight. One dollar."

"*Sí.*"

After he had stowed his burlap sack safely in the small kitchen behind the bar, checked his pocket for the five dollar bill, he went outside where Millie was parked on the street. He walked up to the open window and handed Millie the five dollar bill.

"I don't need. He says he knows my Papa. Say he'll take me there after work. I'm fine now, thank you."

"You just don't do things like that. What if he's only sayin'? What if he don't know your Papa at all?"

"Say he sings like bird. That be my Papa. I'm fine now. He say I can wait inside. I'm going now. Thank you." Diego turned to walk away when Millie called. She leaned over and handed the five dollar bill back.

"Here. Keep this. You may need it."

Diego took it, his hands sweaty, and went back into the bar where he hid behind the curtain and watched the street. Millie sat parked there staring straight ahead, her hands gripping the wheel. The dusty curtains made Diego's eyes water, and then Millie started the car, honked once, long and loud, and gunned the car into the street.

"A broken heart?" the bartender asked.

"*Sí*," he whispered, the five dollar bill crumpled in his fist.

Diego was surprised he had not been struck by a thunderbolt. His Papa singing like a bird was one thing, but to say his Mama was dead was blasphemy. *Father Felipe would skin him alive had he heard him confess*, he thought. But he was far from the confession box, farther from anything he had known, farther perhaps from anything he could know. The bartender wanted him to sing, and he would sing, he would sing his hard heart out tonight. He had made a lie live, and his Papa was out there. It was no longer a whim or blurred truth to a stranger. He wanted to find him. His father had not died. He remembered there was no coffin. No fall from a rooftop.

"You look all done in," the bartender. "Why don't you rest up and stretch out," he motioned to the kitchen. "There's some biscuits left from breakfast. Help yourself. I'm Earl," he said saluting with the towel. "Can't wait to see what the cowboys will make of you," and he bent his head to rinsing and drying whiskey glasses.

"Pedro. I'm Pedro."

"Well, Pedro, glad to know ya. Hope you know some Texas

songs. The cowboys are big on Texas."

"Sure. Sure I know," and Diego, weary, dragged himself into the kitchen.

It was small, only big enough for a stove, upon which chili simmered, a narrow sink, a refrigerator dressed in yellowed newspaper clippings depicting the history of the bar, and a broken bar stool which leaned against the wall. Sacks of beans were heaped in the far corner, and Diego noticed with relief a screen door opening into the alley. He opened his sack, sat upon the bags of beans and took out the ribs and biscuits Millie had made the night before. *She would be back*, he thought. *She did not easily give up.* The ribs were sweet, and he ate with relish even though the morning had only recently waned. He would sing tonight, maybe tomorrow, but he had to keep going. It was good to know he could work, could pocket some money, but he didn't know about cowboys, and he knew only a few Texas songs.

He stood and placed his mouth beneath the faucet and drank. He had begun to sweat. The kitchen was steamy from the simmering chili, and not a wisp of air issued from the door. He sat down again on the beans, punching them into a pillow and lay down. A radio played music in the bar, and the songs drifted lazily on the hot air. They were Texas songs, and Diego was suddenly alert, humming the melody, struggling with the words until he had five songs memorized, and then he fell as if from the lucky sky, into sleep.

He woke groggy, his shirt stained with sweat.

Earl heard him stirring and turned from where he had been stirring the chili.

"Ya slept all day. Thought I might have had to call the coroner," and he laughed showing white, square teeth.

Diego sat up alarmed. He did not know *coroner*, but the way Earl's grim smile turned his lips down at the corners made him shiver. He reached for his sack, stuck his hand in, felt the smooth rectangle of the Diamond Tips box, and let out a breath. He stood, close to Earl now in the small room. "I have Texas songs and some Mexican."

"Hope ya do boy. The cowboys here are quite particular. More so when they're drunk. Save your Spanish songs for late. They'll be so blasted by then and won't care."

"*Sí*." Diego eased around Earl's broad back. "Your restroom, *señor* ?"

"Through the bar on the left," Earl sputtered. "And don't be goin' all Mexican on me. *Sí* and *señor*. The boys don't like it. Pedro is Mexican enough."

Diego slipped past the bar, his burlap sack in tow, and went into the bathroom. The door didn't close all the way, and he was hesitant about taking off his shirt in case the bartender came looking for him. He turned the faucets, and soon a wave of warm water filled his hands. He splashed his face and took paper towels from a metal box and dabbed at his neck and under his arms where a sour metallic smell had taken hold. His face had seemed to grow longer, more like his father's, and his brown eyes looked back at him with confidence. He could do this. He could sing the cowboys under the table. He could have something they wanted. Maybe Millie would be there. If it were at all possible, she would understand. After all, he hadn't burned her barn, and maybe she knew all along, maybe she had seen the pile of straw kicked away.

They came in in ones and threes and then fives. They were a tough bunch, weathered and calloused, demanding their beer in a shrill Texan drawl. Some sat at the few small tables set before the wooden palettes that served as a stage, their legs spread, their boots scuffed. The others, their elbows gripped on the bar, drank whiskey like it was water. Diego stood at the door to the kitchen. Earl had told him to keep scarce until he went on. Women came in in shiny blouses and full skirts. Earl set them up with red liquor with pink paper umbrellas. They smiled and sipped their drinks surveying the crowd. Swirls of cigarette smoke wafted above them like a veil.

Diego had seen pretty girls, girls with straight, white teeth and tempting curves. The Mexican girls kept to themselves, were not allowed at dances. But the white girls went wherever they wished, owning the land. Diego hadn't followed when a white girl turned to him and beckoned for him to follow. The laws of the land were not made for the Mexicans, and he was not stupid. But he did look. These girls in the bar were only shadows pretty, older, with sallow skin unlike all the shades of brown of his people. The girl with the blue blouse returned his scrutiny.

"Hey, Earl. Think you're harboring a Tom peeper."

"Oh him," Earl said, waving Diego back in the kitchen. "He's the entertainment tonight. Harmless Sukie, A kitten. You'll see."

"Cute," she said and turned, her eyes still fixed on Diego. She ran her hand across a cowboy's back. "Hey Tommy, ain't he cute?"

The cowboy stirred, drink in hand, and stared at Diego. "A real peasant if you ask me," and he turned away, gulping his beer.

"Maybe he can sing," and she turned and was lost in the crowd, only the blue shiny shirt glimmered here and there.

Other men and women came into the bar, a few in fine shirts and trousers, a few in sleeveless flowered dresses. The room was stagnant, and Diego cleared his raspy throat and stood a moment at the door to the alley. He could run. Grab his bag and run. Hitch a ride to God knows where. Maybe walk back to Millie's farm. The chili was steaming again. Clean bowls were stacked in the sink. He had not eaten since Millie's ribs.

An old man, his skin dark as ebony, entered the bar and the cowboys cheered.

Stamping their boots and holding their drinks high, they chanted.

"Smokin' Joe. Smokin' Joe. Smokin' Joe."

"Pedro. Come on. You're on," Earl called into the kitchen. "Get out here for chrissakes before they break up the place."

The old man took his place at the piano and his fingers danced across the keys.

Time passed. Earl dimmed the lights. The cowboys, their hats cocked, their legs unsteady beneath them, made their way to the bar for a last splash and clink of ice. Earl motioned to Diego, who stood frozen at the kitchen door, his fingers locked on the sill.

"It's time," he said.

Diego, his throat raw from the smoke, grasped a half-filled glass from the bar, drank it down, and walked through the crowd to the stage. The boards creaked under his feet. He cleared his throat and saluted the crowd. There was a great stomping and laughter and a slight flurry of clapping. The girl in the blue blouse sat near the stage on a cowboy's lap, her legs crossed, her foot kicking the stale air.

"*Buenos noches*," he said. Diego lowered his head to his chest and began to sing "*San Antonio Rose*," and the old man accompanied him. This was a song he knew from the cowboys at the ranch. He sang it mournfully as it was supposed to be sung as if his mother lay breathless before him, her body lifeless on the kitchen table, her dusty shoes dangling. Lifeless from the lie he had told with no one to build her coffin, his sisters bereft and alone. He sang all the many choruses. He was about to sing the final chorus in Spanish, for he knew both, when he looked up at the girl in the blue blouse, her leg still, but he checked himself and sang on until he whispered the final words. "Well, that moonlit pass by the Alamo, And rose my rose of San Antone!"

The crowd stilled, quiet as a tumbleweed across the barroom floor, and then as if the Rio Grande had crashed onto shore, the crowd broke into loud, raucous cheers. It was then Diego knew, small in the dim light, that he would not leave Texas. He would travel to its borders, but not cross the line.

Diego sang, reaching for the foreign notes, his eyes closed, a flame burst inside, slow and flickering. As it grew the flame became an inferno. He saw his stepfather in the faces of the cowboys, not Mexican, but crude and brutal. He heard his stepfather's voice calling for his dolly, his rough hands clenching the small of his back, the humiliation.

He sang the Texas songs, the songs he had learned on the radio, sweet and proud.

The flame grew. He saw the barn on fire, the flames licking the rafters, the horses nickering wildly, the rutted lane beneath his feet, his pants barely hitched, the blood trickling between his legs as red as his shame, his burlap sack slapping his legs as he ran.

He sang the "Yellow Rose of Texas" in Spanish for it was a favorite among Mexicans too.

He was unsure whether his stepfather had been inside, whether his skin had licked flame, turned black and fell from him like snakeskin. He had been near the barn.

The crowd burst forth like volcano fire when he sang, "and the yellow rose of Texas shall be mine evermore." He bowed under the heat, though he felt faint, and growled, "*Gracias, gracias. Buenas noches.*"

The fury within him to make fire was so great he rushed to the kitchen, grabbed his sack, and hurried out into the night. He ran down the alley, crossing and crisscrossing paths, his heart hammering in his chest as a fiery pain engulfed him. He heard his father call out, "Slow down, slow down, Diego." He tripped over a rusted can and bit his lip to keep from crying. He knelt on the ground, gathering wisps of grass and weed and cried, "O my dear Angel Guardian, preserve me from the misfortune of offending God." His fingers trembled as the match was struck, his heart beating like a galloping horse. The grass took slowly, climbing like a spider web up the pyramid of grass he had built. It flamed until it fell back upon itself and crumbled into soft red ember. A calm spread like the endless plains, a relief. When all was blackness, Diego rubbed his hand in the ash. He drew a mark in the center of his forehead with the black soot as they did on Ash Wednesday, gazing into the past and confronting the future. He knew neither time nor day. When he struggled to his feet, the fire still streaking through his chest, he threaded his way to the Prairie Run Bar. He recalled the streaks of dust tracks across the barroom floor, the smear of beer foam across the tables, but he saw only the stage where he had summoned his voice. He would go back for the dollar owed. He would face the bartender with his palm out. *He could make a living with songs,* he thought, and this comforted him. He knew when he was singing that he could strive for higher notes, create a swagger in the rhythms, have them reeling.

He stopped at the bar's back door, wiped the ash from his forehead, and entered. Earl stood, his back to him, washing the bowls that he had served up. He turned. "Pedro, where the hell have ya been? Ya had them in the palm of your hand. Ya should have stayed. Gone on for another set. Never seen such a tamed Friday night crowd."

Diego put his hand out. "Dollar."

"Ya only sang half the night. Fifty cents," and he dug in his pockets until he fished out two quarters.

"I sing two sets, that's two dollars. One set, one dollar," Diego said, shaking the quarters in his palm.

"Okay. Okay," Earl said, digging again in his pockets. He slapped the quarters into Diego's hand. "There, we're even. To-morrow's the big night. The place'll be ripe with cowboys, ripe for a fight. Do what you did tonight, lull 'em to sleep."

"I will sing them to heaven."

"Good. Now get in there and sweep up. Here's a rag for them tables."

"*Sí,*" Diego said as he watched Earl take the money box from the bar and scurry into the kitchen.

Diego took the broom and the rag. The barroom tables were still littered with amber ashtrays filled with cigars and cigarettes. He emptied these into a dustbin at the corner of the bar. A few stray glasses, the ice long since melted, stood in watery pools. He set these on the counter before drinking the stale contents and wiped down the tables. Humming *"Celito Lindo,"* he swept the dust into the street. As he stood in the night watching the sparse traffic squirrel through the city, Earl came to stand beside him.

"Pedro. There was an old woman looking for a Mexican boy. She described him real good, but you'd left."

"What did you say?"

"That you'd moved on," and Earl took the broom from Diego's hand and stood in the doorway. "You tore them up tonight. Best get some sleep. There's some chili left if you want some. I'm gonna lock up. You can sleep in the kitchen."

Diego sang for the next several nights, sleeping on the sacks of beans in the kitchen, smelling the chili or pot stew Earl made for his customers. The need for fire subsided but, like a cat, he heard the cowboy's silver lighters click open and saw the flame, and he was wary. He sang louder then, sang the popular songs that he learned on the radio during the day, hitting a wrong note or word which made the cowboy's laugh, and the girls put their hands to their mouths. He sang with closed eyes, his arms doing a dance of their own, beseeching. In the morning he asked for his dollars and hid them in his bag which he kept close. He washed his clothes and his body in the bathroom sink, hung his clothes in the alley to dry and was grateful to Millie for the plentiful clothes. He dried himself on the kitchen step, sunning himself in the Texas sun.

During the days he ran errands for Earl, sweeping, washing dishes, marketing, exploring. Sweetwater was an oil boom town, and the metal structures that erased the horizon littered the land. Jacks, like pumping prehistoric creatures, commanded the rural parts of town. He did not spend his money, secreting a dime or quarter Earl had given him for shopping. He loitered around the lumberyard and hardware store hoping for a glimpse of his father, and once, when he asked a burly clerk if Manuel Ramirez had been there, the man growled.

"You think I take note of every wetback that sneaks into this town?" and he swept angrily at the counter. "If you ain't buyin', then git out."

Diego left but stood to watch the men coming and going outside on the sidewalk. His head buzzed and melted with the liquor he had drunk from half-empty glasses. He wondered which route his father might have taken. Diego guessed he would not go far, that he would go with the work. A carpenter was important to these boom towns. He would be with the work. Diego would find him like a penitent seeking a priest. As he was musing, the clerk came out and shouted.

"I tole you to git. Now git, or I'll call the law for loiterin'."

Diego sang for the next several nights. The girl with the blue blouse taunted him from the cowboys' laps, but she wore red and coral and then emerald. The cowboys got drunk and brawled among themselves. Earl easily dropped them onto the sidewalk when they became too rowdy. Drinks were spilled, glasses broke, and ashtrays were overturned. Chili steamed from the kitchen and bowls were emptied, and Diego sang, his eyes closed to the commotion. He learned how to steel himself from the drunken jaws thrust from the cowboys' faces. The making of fires seemed far away, but in the far reaches of the night when the bar had emptied, he clutched for his matches in his sleep. In these quiet spells where he moved and talked as if in a dream, sometimes he let himself wonder about fire. He had looked for Millie, but it seemed she had heeded Earl's message that he had moved on: and he had. He sang now, but not so long ago, he had set to burning her barn. He would have, too, if she had not startled him. He sang now, not getting too close, trying to put as much distance from himself and others. Even Earl had questioned him.

"Pedro? Where are you off to? I just tole you to wash them bowls. They won't do it themselves," and he flicked his towel at the kitchen sink. "You're about as much company as a ghost." He flicked his towel again, and Diego listened as Earl mounted the steps to his room.

Diego hungered for the calm of his remoteness. It kept the fire thoughts at bay. It gave him a place where he could savor his newly found talents. He was a man earning his way. He hid his dollars in his sack, and he swelled as they did.

He sang through the next week, his dollars becoming thick. Each day he wandered the streets and alleyways. He passed the remains of his fire, crossed himself, feeling like dead ash, strong and cold, and patted his burlap sack where he secreted his matches. When he sang, he no longer saw his stepfather's face among those of the cowboys. He believed he had conquered his nightmares. He even laughed along when the drunks stumbled over each other on their way to the bar for a refill. He sang sweetly and lulled the most rackety drunks.

One Saturday night, the girl with the blue dress entered. It was late. He was singing his last set. She found a cowboy, leaned against his arm and teased Diego, flashing looks at him from across the room. She was not wearing the blue blouse but a filmy blouse the color of yellow rice. He noticed she was older than he'd thought with fine lines along her mouth and eyes. Her eyes looked pouched and raw. She made up for the late hour by downing her drinks quickly, laughing harshly, calling to Earl from where she stood.

"Earl? Are you running a saloon or what?" and she'd hold out her glass until Earl came around the bar with a fresh one. She sashayed up to Diego, swaying uncertainly, her drink sloshing onto the floor. "Pedro? Sing me a love song."

Diego had watched her coming. He also watched the cowboy upon whom she'd been draped. The cowboy sat up straighter and shook his head. He laughed privately with his buddies staring bullets at Diego.

"*Señorita,* only lullabies."

"Then sing me to sleep," and she pulled at Diego's pants. The bar burst into laughter. Her cowboy stood. Diego began a haunting old lullaby his mother had sung to him when he couldn't sleep. He did not close his eyes. He kept them riveted on the cowboy and his friends who had risen and now stood on the edge of the platform where he sang. When he had sung the last words and given the audience his *buenas noches*, he stepped away from the crowd that had formed.

"Another!" the cowboy growled reaching uncertainly for Diego's sleeve. The good shirt Millie had given him tore.

"A love song. The lady wants a love song," the other men shouted.

Earl, shouting too, wove his way through the crowd. "Last call!"

The girl with the yellow blouse threw her head back, gulped her drink and chased after Earl. "Another scotch and soda!"

Mindful of closing, the men soon broke up, but the girl's cowboy stood his ground by Diego.

"You want some don't you?"

"I know no love songs."

"I suppose you think she's pretty."

"*Señor* it is late. You want your drink. It soon is closing."

The cowboy was a full head taller than Diego. The cowboy rocked with drink. His face was ugly.

"She wants a love song. Sing."

Diego surveyed the room. Most of the crowd was clustered around the bar getting their last drinks.

"I said sing, you sawed off Mexican rat," and he lunged for Diego but not before Diego had landed a two-fisted punch in the cowboy's gut. Diego watched as the cowboy folded on the floor, and then he ran as fast as he could into the kitchen, grabbed his sack and sped off into the night. As he ran, he felt for his matches, but he did not feel like making fire. He knuckles stung where he had met the cowboy's buckle. Diego hoped they had bled.

Chapter 5:
The Dark Priest

The fist connecting with flesh left Diego fireless. He ran in the hot night. Sweat poured down his ribs. Heat consumed him but without match or flame. His shirt was soaked. He passed lightless cottages. He heard dogs barking, but he ran, fearless. He could not go back. His songs, his voice, trailed after him, winding out in a long thin cloud, lace. He was a small boy, but he felt larger than the night sky. He would leave this city of sweet water never having tasted its balm of which his father had boasted. The chance that he would meet his father here was gone. He would move on. He felt no sadness. He felt for his map. He looked forward to the next driver.

As he left the maze of streets and alleyways, he saw a car standing at the curb. Its lights were on, the engine hummed. It was as if luck had finally found Diego, and he approached cautiously, his euphoria speeding out ahead of him. He tapped on the glass.

Long moments passed before the door opened.

"I would like to hitch," Diego queried. "To Abilene? Are you going?"

The figure in the car motioned him in. Diego settled himself in the seat, pressing his sack between his legs, and the car sped off. He wanted to speak and felt a great stream of words, some Spanish, some English crowding his tongue. He wanted to tell this dark man in the dark clothes of his dollars and the lullabies, of Earl and Millie and the salesman. He wanted to speak of his adventures, his many braveries, but the man beside him was silent. He wanted him to know the dark deeds that had taken place with his stepfather. He wanted him to know his hunger, the quench of fire. He wanted all this but could not break the stillness. It was as if this journey with the quiet, dark man were preordained. He could hear Father Felipe chiding him, inciting him to speak, but he could not. Every time he opened his mouth, it was with a rush, like the mighty Rio Grande, and Diego fell silent too.

The air was stifling, and Diego cracked the window open. The man turned then and looked at him as if noticing Diego for the first time. His clothes were black. A black cowboy hat sat awry on his head. The few lights from the dashboard didn't illuminate his dark face. His hands clenched the wheel. The driver's stillness and appearance reminded Diego of a charred log, one Diego had set on fire. He had returned and returned to this log, chiseling in its char, soiling pants by sitting on its black remains, trying to pry the meaning of its death. Diego's neck prickled with sweat and sudden fear.

"You can let me off here," Diego said, but the car sped on.

Perhaps the driver had not heard, and Diego repeated his request. The man looked neither left nor right. Diego thought the car drove itself as it wove its way into the night, the man a mere chunk of blackened wood. Diego thought he would touch him, but feared the black cloth crumbling like ash beneath his hand, the car veering into the brush. Tumbleweeds blew across the road, and the wheels crushed them, sending up a fine spray of chaff.

After many miles, Diego spoke again.

"I'm tired. I sleep now," and Diego turned toward the door, resting his head against the metal, feeling every bump in the road. He only feigned sleep and expected at any moment for the car to swerve off the highway into some hidden glen where he would meet the maker Father Felipe talked about. His knuckles oozed blood where he had met with the cowboy's buckle at the bar. It had seemed so long ago but was perhaps only hours. He was not prepared for another fight. The euphoria he had felt had dissipated like mist on a Texas morning. He felt small. He put his hand on the door's handle and considered jumping, but the car was going so fast, he knew he would be hurt. His unease was so great, he did not think of fire at all.

Diego felt the man move in his seat. It was almost imperceptible, a soft groaning, a slight shift. Diego thought of the salesman, of his fear of falling asleep. He knew they were traveling fast, that it would only take a moment to swoon into death. He turned and looked at the man. Though he would not touch the man, Diego began to whisper. He told him of fire, a tower of fire, that devastated everything as if to strike fear in the man's dark personage.

"It flickers first, like a candle. Sweet like a melody. It falls in on itself, curling and twisted. Red embers glow. Sparks light. New fire begins. It climbs like a baby at first, tumbling down, then growing fierce. Angry fire, an angry child shouting. It climbs. It takes hold. Then all is flowing up, glowing, brilliant. Sound, crackling is everywhere. Beautiful. So beautiful you must step away. It dances before you, carrying you, filling you. Filling you," Diego's voice faltered, grasping for more words, "Filling you."

The man was a stone, unmoved. He did not slow his car. They drove on in silence until Diego saw the glittering lights of a city. Diego would check his map. He would find himself. He laughed at his fears, laughed secretly at the dark man, laughed because he had shared his most precious secret. It was the middle of the night. The city would not awaken for hours. Though they had entered the city, the man had not slowed as if he meant to continue driving through the night.

Carefully, so as not to touch the man's arm, Diego tugged at the man's shirt.

"I must go now," and Diego motioned to the door in the same manner that the dark man had ushered him into the car. The car slowed. Diego opened the door and climbed out, his sack tucked under his arm.

"*Gracias,*" Diego called into the night as the car was already speeding down the street.

Chapter 6:
Sylvie the Night Walker

"Hey, doll, you okay?"

Diego's head rose from where it was snug against his neck.

"Doll?" she said, bending over him, her black rhinestone bag dragging on the pavement.

There it was again. *Doll. Dolly. My dolly.*

"You're gonna get rolled, Doll, If you ain't got sense," she said straightening.

He rose unsteadily, the unfinished drinks he had drunk and the long drive finally taking their toll.

"Doll, you sick or something?"

And that had done it. His arms swung wide, and the girl caught them in both her hands.

"Do I look like a thug?" she said, twisting his arms into a rope until they hurt. "Thought you might need a doctor is all."

Finally, Diego's mouth curled into slow, snarled words. "Don't say it?"

"Don't say what?"

"Doll. Don't call me your doll."

"You got a broken heart? I can fix that real good."

"I'm good."

"Don't look too good."

"No. I'm good. Just don't call me your doll." Saying the word made Diego hungry for fire.

"You gotta name?"

"Pedro."

"Well, Pedro. The cops sweep this street every two hours. Now you can slump yourself back on the pavement and wait until they pick you up, or you can come with me." She loosened her grip on Diego's arms. "You gonna be a good boy or what?"

"I'm sorry."

"Be sorry on someone's else's dime. I've got work to do." She let his arms swing free, and they slapped into Diego's sides. "I guess you spent all your fire." Her high heels clicked on the sidewalk as she walked away.

"No wait!" he called, running awkwardly after her.

She looked over her shoulder.

"You already cost me. You'd better have some cash."

"I have."

She stopped then, smiled, something veiled coming over her thin, narrow face.

"Amigo, you just found your girl," and she waited for him to catch up and locked her arm in his. Her arms were bare and black like burnt wood. There was a tear in the hem of her pink skirt. "You sure you ain't sick or something? I sure as hell don't need no sickness."

"No sickness. Tired only. Came up from Sweetwater tonight."

"Well. Well. A traveling man. I like that." She stroked his arm. "It ain't much farther. A block or so."

Diego's stomach churned with the fire. He could stop, let her go on about her business, find some prairie grass to rest in. He could hear the Diamond Tips rustling against each other in their box.

"Maybe I find a place to sleep," Diego stammered.

"You'll sleep good at my place. Rest easy." She clutched his arm tighter.

"Half a block."

Diego was used to making his own way. There was something about the girl that didn't set well.

"I ain't just a fly by night girl resting on the Jake's good graces. Got my own place. My own business. He don't need to know a thing about us. You know what I mean?" and she turned and faced Diego and winked. "We're here." She led the way into a narrow alley. A bare bulb illuminated the far end of the passage.

"I'll rest here," Diego said, lowering himself to the bare dirt. His sack slung over his shoulder.

"What! You think mebbe I be a street whore. Where you come from? A barn or something!"

The smell of smoldering horseflesh, the barn doors crackling, the panicked whinnies cascaded.

"Get up!" she screamed. "Get out of my alley!" And she slung her bag over her shoulder and swung it at Diego's head. It hit him with a wild slap, rhinestones scattering to the ground.

She gathered the strap and cried, "My good bag! You've about wasted what's left of the night! Go on. Get out! Get out!" Her high heels scudding on the rich brown earth, she raced down the alley where the bare bulb lit her small brown body. She paused and looked toward where Diego still sat and shouted. "Don't you be there in the morning," she said as she fumbled with her keys she let herself into the building and disappeared.

Diego fought the desire for fire and the need for sleep, and sleep won.

He woke to suffocating heat and the sound of traffic. His head buzzed with booze and fatigue. A barrel stuffed with a broken rocking chair said, TRASH ONLY. He stood shaky and confused. He could remember a girl and rhinestones but no more. The alley was empty. He remembered horses but nothing more. He walked to the barrel and urinated. He knew he would make fire today and took two of the barrel's broken wooden slats, stuffed them into his bag and walked into the street.

Chapter 7:
Senorita's Gown

Diego felt swamped by the breadth of Abilene. It was hot and dry, and the buildings dwarfed him. He stopped in a bodega for a loaf of bread and an orange Fanta. Cars and trucks cluttered the roads and would not stop for him. He passed the pumping jacks and large rectangular buildings whose metal reflected the sharp glare of the sun, big rigs, chain link fence. His head felt swollen. His shirt, the good one from out of Millie's kindness, was soaked with sweat. He sat down on the curb, rolled the bread into his mouth, drank his Fanta, and swore off alcohol. A truck roared by and blasted his horn, but he was not hitchhiking now. Diego cursed him with his finger.

He was not used to the city, and he longed with a keen desperation to find a home for his fire. He followed Route 59 North for what seemed hours until he came to a side road that wound out onto the prairie. There were few houses, and he walked until he could walk no more and sat in the brush. The sun had driven all thought. He was raw, mindless, purposeful, slow, the only way to enjoy a fire. He was so hungry for fire that his hands trembled.

He sat in the brush until the merciless sun disappeared and night settled in. He spoke his prayer, his ode to God, pulled out a match and struck it against the box. The flame was orange at its peak, blue at its base and it had lit a small tuft of tinder. Diego exhaled wearied with waiting. He had not had to use the barrel's staves he had salvaged from the trash. Smug and silent, he thought how he would save them for another time, another fire, though each fire seemed to be his last. The tinder heated quickly, small sparks of fire circling then dying into pinpricks of light. The prairie, the curves like a swollen belly, was strewn with brush left unattended by the oil boom. When the fire caught, it swept eastward in a precise fiery line and moved, though the wind was light, across the land. The moonlit night illuminated the black smoke, and it was as if Diego had loosed a locomotive. He had forgotten the bar fight, Earl, the girl in the blue blouse.

Diego did not hear the man until he was upon him, clutching his shoulders.

"You like fire," the man finally said while Diego struggled futilely. "I like fire too," he said, rolling Diego's shoulders so that he could not see the fire, his head bent and staring at the ground. "It'll burn out soon's it gets to the oilman's reservoir. Just beyond that rise. You got good intentions, but not much sense. I would'a set it about a mile north of here." He roughly turned Diego around until they were facing each other. "Got a name?"

"Pedro!" Diego spat. "It hurts."

"Not half so much were you to set one of those rigs on fire. Now that's a sight." Again the man turned him to face the fire. The fire had fanned out like a crimson senorita's gown. His breath came in short, hot gasps as the swelling in his groin subsided. The wind lifted and turned slightly, and Diego thought it might turn back. He struggled.

"No need. Watch the smoke build, it's dying. Reached the water. The show's over." He shoved Diego gently backward and headed for the road. He called back over his shoulder, "You coming or what, Pedro? Sheriff and trucks will be here soon. You a firecracker or what? Or maybe just plain loco."

"I'll come," Diego called, and quickly he scrambled in the dust for his matchbox and sack and raced after him.

A big, old, rusty Ford was parked in the dirt. The man stood leaning against the door cleaning his teeth with a toothpick. "You from Abilene?" he asked.

"No, El Paso," Diego stammered thinking what a big world it was, how one would not find El Paso, the ranch, how it was almost gone for him too.

"You're a little far from home," he said, scuffing the dirt with his boot. "How old are you?"

"Eighteen,"Diego lied.

"Best we be going then. They catch you up good at 18 and don't let you go. You know that?"

"Yes, Sir."

"How old?"

"Fifteen."

"More like it. Get in," and the man heaved himself forward while Diego slung his sack into the bed of the truck and struggled to climb in.

"Not there," the man said quickly, but Diego had already seen his cargo, boxes and boxes and barrels of books.

"You read all these?"

"Get in," and the man held the door for him while he climbed in. As the man circled around the front of the truck, Diego sensed both the adventure and poverty of his life. He had never shared fire with anyone. It was a solitary ritual. The man had not turned him in, had admitted to liking fire also. Before entering the truck, the man scraped his boots on the fender.

Finally, he sat beside Diego, jangled his keys, selected one, and started the truck which grumbled reluctantly to life.

"Read most of them. The ones with red covers the most. I read those first. Then the green ones, the blue, and the black. I never did finish the yellow ones. "

"Forever?"

"It took a long time. I don't have time now for the yellow ones. The missus threw me out. I'm heading back home."

Diego, who had never been enamored of books, had scarcely been able to read them asked, "Reading, was worthy?"

"You mean, worth it. I suppose. There's a whole lot of sadness in most books, more so in life, I suppose, at least in my life. It's like taking a magnifier and looking at your palm. Reading's like that, uncovers a whole 'nother world."

"What's best?"

"The books with fire," and then he laughed and laughed until he started coughing, and Diego laughed too.

They drove for a while in silence, the thump of tires on uneven pavement the only chorus.

"You sell?" and Diego motioned toward the bed of the truck.

"You gonna buy?"

"No."

"Then I ain't gonna sell. Have a plan for them. You wait and see," and then as he fell silent again, the man seemed to age. His skin got greyer, his jaw drooped, his hands seemed as if they gripped the steering wheel with difficulty. When he finally spoke again, even his voice seemed frail. "Almost there."

Diego looked about. The moon still lit the prairie, but there were no houses, just brush and dried brown grasses. As the road swung up over a slight rise and lowered, the truck slowed. Diego clutched his sack prepared to run. The truck pulled onto a gravel bed and stopped.

"By golly, this is it. I'm certain."

"This is nowhere."

"This, Pedro, is home."

Diego looked about. All he could see was a nest of tumbleweed.

"Beyond that," and he pointed, then climbed out of the truck. Reluctantly Diego also climbed out of the truck. He stood on the gravel bed.

"Nothing."

Then the man scrambled over to the tumbleweed. He grabbed at the weeds with both hands and pulled. He did this again and again, and Diego thought he had met a crazy man. Twenty minutes passed while Diego stood, and the man battled with the tumbleweed. Diego gasped.

"There," he said and beyond the tumbleweed stood a low, flat house, its windows grimed with dust, the front door askew and rusted on its hinges.

"Home Sweet Home," the man laughed.

"You live here?"

"Plan to plant myself down. Needs some sprucing, but yeah, I plan to. Come on give me a hand."

Together they pulled the weeds away from the house. As they worked, the man seemed younger again. They remained silent, grunting, and heaving, and acknowledging thistles with grunts and moans.

When they had uncovered the front of the small clapboard house, the man returned from the truck with a flashlight. He shined the torch on the door, wrested the door from its hinges, and stepped inside. Diego watched at a safe distance, the light ghostly as it shed its swath of light. The man returned to the door.

"Come on," he said, swaying the light across the yard strewn with tumbleweed.

"No. I stay here."

"Christ son, I need your help. I saw your fire and knew you was my boy, my savior. Come on in now. I didn't turn you in. Liked your fire, in fact, smooth like a rolling wave it was. Come on. I'm done in."

Diego dragged his sack across the rubble. The man stood at the doorway, and Diego moved up beside him. The man shined the light into a small dusty room.

"Gonna put my books up here. Go to the truck and bring the

boxes. We'll set the books down here," and he shined his light again.

Diego thought of his mother, her daily struggle with rice and beans, the wash, the chores for the ranch. The man looked tired. His wrist bent under the weight of the flashlight. He leaned against the splintered door jamb.

"Go on."

Diego stumbled to the truck. He pulled out a box of red books, horses and whores dashing off the covers in the faint moonlight, and struggled with them and brought them to the man who waited in the doorway. The man lifted the box of books from Diego's arms and tossed them into the middle of the room.

"Go on, get more."

Diego strode back and forth from the truck to the house watching sailing ships and haunted castles thrown up into the air and landing with a clatter as he carried cartons of green and black books to the man. A small mountain of paper and cardboard littered the room.

"One more thing. Get that can out from behind the seat. We're gonna see a blaze tonight."

Diego retrieved the can and hurried to the man's side.

"You'll make fire?"

"No. I'm gonna leave the honors to you," and the man stepped inside, the can clutched to his chest. He poured the contents of the can over the books.

"It will burn nice," Diego offered.

"Yessir, it surely will," then he poured the remaining gas across his shoulders and down his chest. "Go on now. Get out those Diamond Tips. I know you have them, saw at the fire, light me up for chrissakes."

Diego was high from the close smell of gasoline and the nearness of fire. He stepped into the room and the man shone the light in his face.

"No. Step back. Throw a match into the room and run like hell. Go on now."

Diego stooped and picked up a yellow book, a book the man had not read. The cover was torn, and Diego could not read the words. A man stood next to a red barn. Cattle littered the prairie beyond. Sadness spilled over Diego.

"You have not read this?"

"No."

"Maybe I burned one man, a bad man, not like the one in the picture."

"That's good. Get on with it."

"Maybe you'll read this before you die?" and Diego threw the book at the man's feet.

"Maybe I read this before," he said not reaching for the book. "He was a good man like you say, the man in the book, but he grew a cancer in his brain, so he wets his marriage bed now, can't remember things, days when his arms shake and his hands tremble. It's a sad story. One you'll hide away in the barn, glad it's over. Now, get out those Diamond Tips. They're the best."

And he stooped and picked up the book and threw it at Diego. Diego caught it. The cover with the man, and the barn, and the cattle tore. Diego held it in his hand. He picked up the book and put it in his satchel. He felt for his matches, the box was hard and geometric in his palm.

"I cannot do this," he finally said. He tossed the box of matches to the man, and the lid slid open and the matches with their red tips spilled out at the man's feet.

"Go on then," he threw the keys of the truck to Diego. Diego stared at the keys. He would stop this if he could, but he had thrown the matches. He staggered out into the night. He walked away from the truck, his back to the man and his matches. He tripped over clods of dirt. He wanted to lie down and sleep as if this were a dream his mother could wash away, but he kept walking, waiting for the sound of fire, the great whoosh of air and crackle. In his mind's eye, he could see the tumbleweed burn.

Chapter 8:
Walking Dog

Diego ran down the rutted road, tripping, sailing into the night. He did not think of the man. He did not think of the fire. He did not wait for the rush and whoosh of flame. He thought of the tumbleweed, the ones they had scattered, how they would burn with a magician's precision, each one unique like the snowflakes that sometimes fell. He felt the sadness of missing something important, but he did not think of the man with his skin curling and blackening. He remembered his stepfather, and Diego's face flamed in the night.

After months of the weekly scouring at his stepfather's hands, something had changed like a cataclysmic falling from grace, like a pebble being dropped into water. Diego found if he submitted easily, the beatings lessened, so much so that his mother withheld the extra helping of hated rice and beans.

"Diego, you are getting fat," she had remarked. "You are becoming a man."

Diego was thirteen and like all things chafed over time, he had become tarnished and marked and no longer pleaded silently for his mother to rescue him. Shame, which he wore with a lowered gaze and halting gait, stilled his tongue, and he learned how irrevocably alone he was.

When he emerged, he remembered the thin walls of his home and his mother's wary smile.

As dawn crept along the flat horizon, Diego neared the highway. He did not think of the man or miss the tumbleweed's burning so much. He heard trucks roaring across the prairie, and he cut across the scrub brush, tearing his pants, hungry for movement. When he finally reached the highway, his throat burned with thirst. The road was not heavily trafficked, and Diego sat down by the side of the road to take inventory. He opened his sack and spilled its contents on the ground. His Diamond Tips were gone. Only one match remained, and Diego saw that the sulfur tip was chipped and would probably not light. He greedily drank the remains of the orange Fanta. The yellow book, with its missing cover, he laid gently on his knee. He opened the book to the first remaining page.

"It's a good farm all right when you get the weeds off," it read. He could make out most of the words. He would keep it in his sack and read it when he wasn't hitching. It was a good thing from the man, like the clothes from Millie. He would keep it, and he tucked it back into the sack with his other various scraps of paper he had scavenged along the road. He stuck the empty Fanta bottle in his pant pocket bent on filling it with water at the first sign of a gas station. He stood and began to walk north along the highway, his feet scuffing through the gravel. He had walked for a mile or two when he turned his body to face the oncoming traffic. A car and a truck, the only motorists he had seen yet this morning, sped past him. The truck sped up along the road, the other vehicle slowed and pulled into the grass about a hundred feet ahead. It carried a horse in a rusted trailer. An arm was stuck out of the driver's window and motioned to Diego to hurry up. Diego ran, his bag slapping against his legs, almost tripping him.

The car was old, the door strung closed with a coat hanger, the window missing.

"You a calf roper?" the Indian smiled, his broad face beaming.

"No."

"Not a bronco buster?"

"No," and Diego laughed. "I am just along the road."

"Not horse shit, no?"

"No," Diego smiled and laughed again.

"Then get in. I don't need the competition anyway."

Diego struggled with the door when the Indian laughed.

"Through the window gringo," and he laughed, and Diego thrust his bag inside, and pulled himself into the car. The seats were threadbare, and there were spots where tufts of horsehair showed through. The Indian smelled like the burning sun, and Diego liked him right away.

"I am Pocahontas. My show name, a distraction while I thrust and tug and tie my knots. I'm a calf roper and bull rider. There's a rodeo up aways. Where you going?"

"The rodeo. I'll come too." Rodeos in Texas were a common event and though Diego had never gone to one before, he was caught up in the Indian's excitement.

"You got money?"

"Some," Diego said.

"You'll need money," and he slapped his pocket. "Right here. Tie my knots, ride the bronco and I come home with a cool four hundred. Not bad, eh?"

"Good money."

"The best." The car had begun to tremble beneath them. "Overheating, best get going. What's your name?"

"Pedro," Diego said quietly.

"Well, Pedro. I'm only four hundred bucks away from hootch and some white pussy," and he eased the throbbing car onto the road. The car bucked and backfired. "You'll have to excuse me while I tend to Bessie," and he tapped the cracked and dusty dashboard. "She doesn't like hearing about any other women, jealous she is." The Indian talked softly then, a chant almost or a lullaby, caressing the side of the car through the open window. "Baby, baby, come on now, don't say it's quits. I love you too," and the engine evened out, and the car began to pick up speed. The Indian looked over at Diego and winked. "Pays to be nice otherwise there's hell."

Diego tried to settle into the broken seat. Every time he leaned back the seat folded back with a thud.

"Just let it stay back. It's broke for sure. What do you do besides walk along the road like horse shit?"

"I sing. I am a singer."

"Good?"

"I am good. They pay for my singing."

"Then you are good," the Indian swerved around a dead coyote. "You looking for work?"

"Always. I sing in bar, but cowboy punch me. He thinks I took to his girl."

"Was he right?"

"Maybe," and they both laughed, the car alive with their laughter. "What's your name?"

"My Indian name or the one the school gave me?"

"Your name. What you like to be called?"

"Walking Dog."

"It's a good name. Walking Dog. I like it even if I fear dogs. We had mean dogs at the ranch."

"Around here?"

"No. El Paso. Far away."

"I'll say. Look, Pedro. I'll need someone to brush out Tonto," and he motioned to the horse trailer in back, "Cheer me on. If you do good work, I'll help you find some singing. Deal?"

"Sí," Diego said, feeling at every moment his sorrow lifting as if the man had not burned himself, had not given the yellow book to Diego in parting, a book he had not read.

A few miles up the road, the traffic snarled in two straight lines, north and south, all struggling with their trailers of horses, calves and bulls, all trying to gain the rodeo entrance. Bessie slowed, billowing acrid, blue smoke.

"Smoke will kill Tonto," and he waved to his horse whinnying in the trailer. "Hold on." While traffic inched forward, Walking Dog pulled into the empty, southbound lane. "I'm gonna try an old Indian trick." He slung his arm out the side of the car and slapped the side in a bam bam Indian rhythm crying in a sharp, shrill voice, "A Ti Yi Yippee Yippee Yi, Yippee Yi, a Ti Yi Yippee Yippee Yi." He repeated this over and over again until he reached the entrance to the rodeo. Bessie smoked and strained. Tonto's whinny could be heard above Walking Dog's sing song cry.

A cowboy, dressed in leather chaps and a red fringed shirt, stood in the road. Before he had a chance to shout, Walking Dog edged Bessie into the dirt lane.

"Gates of heaven. Here we are," he called back to the attendant smiling, Bessie slowing.

"Get that heap out of here!" the attendant shouted.

Walking Dog hit the gas, and Bessie rumbled over the uneven gravel.

"Works every time," Walking Dog laughed. "They don't want a jam up."

"You always so brave?"

"Now that's a word I haven't heard in a long time."

They passed sorry looking wooden buildings, corrals, swayback fences, and the grandstand. Fields surrounded the rodeo proper, and Walking Dog steered Bessie into the clearing, choosing a spot that was even and faced away from the grandstand.

"Don't want Tonto to get fired up too soon. Let's get him out of there. We've been driving three hours. He'll be hungry and need his kinks ironed out."

Diego climbed out of the window and met Walking Dog at the back of the trailer.

"Don't spook him. Talk sweet. Get in there and unlatch his

tether, then just ease him out. Can you do that?"

"*Sí*," Diego hummed a lullaby, one he had sung at the bar, and squeezed in between the horse and the trailer. Tonto stamped his foot and shifted uneasily.

"Keep singing. He likes that. Just push on past his belly."

Diego hummed and did as Walking Dog said. He kept humming while Tonto arched his neck and pulled against the rope that tied him to the wall of the trailer.

"No sudden moves," Walking Dog called. "He spooks."

Diego slid his hand along the horse's cheek. Sweat dripped down Diego's face. He unlatched the halter, and Tonto reared back as if to sit.

"Hold onto him and pull back on the rope. Grab his halter. Don't let him slip."

Diego hummed in Tonto's ear, grabbed the halter and as Walking Dog lowered the ramp, he edged him backwards into the clearing.

"Well done. He usually takes out a knee with strangers."

"I think so too," Diego panted as he handed Tonto's rope to Walking Dog.

Walking Dog laughed, "Yup, you'll do," he said, appraising Diego. Diego still hummed raggedly; he shook, and the sweat rolled under his arms and wet the shirt Millie had given him. "You've worked with horses before?"

"Some," Diego lied.

Walking Dog dropped the rope, and Diego started forward and grabbed it.

"You can drop the rope. He'll be ground tied until the calf roping." He slapped Tonto's side, and the horse shied away. "Like I said, he spooks, but in the ring he's cream. Getting him out of that crate," and he pointed to the rusted trailer, "is the hardest."

Walking Dog marched across the scrub grass toward the grandstand, and Diego followed.

"You sing like a sage sparrow and proved yourself with Tonto too. Let's get some grub, and I'll square things up for your singing.

A little hot sauce in Hector Small's chili, and he'll be croaking by half past eight. He loves the stuff, but it makes him hoarser than a hen. You'll be the evening entertainment."

"Do you ride the bull tonight?"

"Barrel racing's tonight. Gets the crowd warmed up. The big events are tomorrow and Sunday."

Men were unloading bulls into a long narrow pen.

"These your bulls?"

"Maybe," Walking Dog grinned as the bulls danced and kicked up dust before them.

Myriad concessions had opened up spiriting everything from tamales to steaming coffee urns. A hot wind carrying sage dust blew in from the west carrying the scent of chili powder and hot peppers. Diego's stomach rumbled, and he searched his sack for the dollars he had earned at the Prairie Run. Walking Dog had a cup full of chili, and Diego feasted on a meat enchilada.

"How much they pay for singing?" Diego said between bites.

"Don't know yet. It depends on how soon Hector falls. I'll introduce you later."

The air was full of neighing, and shouts, and the lowing of angry bulls. Behind them, a trailer was unloading horses into a large corral with roped off stalls.

"They're the broncs, mostly from Rough Riders Ranch. Those horses are a mean bunch. You're wise to be wary. Had a hunk taken out of my arm when I was a kid. Tonto's a calf roper, a different breed altogether. One's bred for an ornery nature, other's bred for his cooperation. Tonto's the cooperative kind, swift and sure. He can kick you square in the chest with one of his hooves, but he don't bite."

"That is good news," Diego soberly smiled, and they both broke into laughter.

As they walked around the grounds, finely dressed cowboys hailed Walking Dog, asked after his mother, his brothers and sisters, and Tonto.

"You still riding that old swayback," they jested.

"You bet," Walking Dog said. "You still riding that cow?"

It made Diego proud to be with Walking Dog, to be under his protection as if a little of Walking Dog's swagger had rubbed off on him. He thought about his sisters. When he left, he worried about them, but they were safe. He had seen his stepfather step into the burning barn. Diego had seen to that. He thought of the man who had liked fire, who no longer wanted to live. Diego had not looked back but wondered if the man had struck the Diamond Tips. Diego knew it was not a good way to die, that is why he chose it for his stepfather.

"Why so somber, partner?"

"I have been long awake is all."

"Let's get back to Tonto. You can brush him down. Then we'll take a little siesta. You'll want to be ripe for the singing tonight and for the girls. Oh my, the pretty *señoritas*."

Diego two-stepped around Tonto's ever-shifting hooves, a brush in hand. The horse's flesh quivered under his gentle strokes. When his coat was gleaming, Diego laid down the brush. "He is clean now," he said.

"Looks smart. Good job," he said, slapping Diego on the back. "We'll let Hector sing the first few bars of the opening tonight, then you'll finish up."

"I like to sing."

"Do ya know any cowboy songs?"

"Plenty. The bar I was singing had only cowboys. They rope me if I sing anything else."

"Good. Start out with something sweet, Home on the Range, something that will tear at their heartstrings. Cowboys are suckers for sweethearts and sage." Walking Dog turned slightly, his face blanched by the sun. "He's here. Hector. Act Mexican."

Diego reached for the brush and stood as close to Tonto as he dared.

"Well, hey, Hector. You dandied up for the night?" Walking Dog teased. Hector wore a brilliant, ruffled, white cowboy shirt, black jeans, and silver filigreed cowboy boots. "I see you polished your spurs."

Hector, a short, squat man with silver hair that contrasted sharply with his black cowboy hat, moved quickly, turning, to inspect his spurs.

Satisfied, he turned to Walking Dog, "I ain't gonna take no guff. Singing clear through 'til Sunday."

"Well, if it pleases you, my hired hand makes a mean chili. Perhaps you could come over before you sing."

Hector regarded Diego, then spat on the ground, "No hot sauce?"

"No," and Diego grabbed his belly. "No hot sauce."

"Good then. If his chili is as good as you say, I'll leave two passes for the grandstand." He tipped his hat and waddled away.

Walking Dog waited until Hector had disappeared into the crowd and then asked Diego, "Can you make a fire?"

"*Sí*," Diego smiled, and they hauled a stack of wood from the trailer.

"I've got to register for the events. You get a fire going, and when I get back, we'll get the chili cooking."

Diego nodded and watched Walking Dog mingle with the other cowboys and then head for the registration booth.

It was good wood, dry, and well seasoned. It smelled of the prairie and tickled his nose.

He dug a small pit with his hands, rimming it with rocks and pebbles. The earth was mostly bare, the grass trampled or scorched away. He took a handful of the scarce grass and placed it in the well he had dug. There was little in the way of kindling. He towered the logs Walking Dog had brought, then searched Bessie for his bag. He found one remaining match. He thought of the waste, his box of Diamond Tips scattered over the books, the tumbleweed that had obliterated the house, the man standing, drenched in gasoline. It was a bad match, the sulfur chipped away. It was all he had now, and his mind flared like forest fire. His hand shook as he neared the pit. Tonto whinnied. It was the first time he did not invoke his guardian angel prayer.

As Tonto struck his hooves on the bare, hard earth, he struck the match against a stone. It flared then whimpered, then flared again. He eased the match toward the prairie grass, and it lit sending spirals of flame that licked the dry wood. Tendrils of bark and wood caught, then faltered then caught again. It was the interplay between air and fire that Diego loved most. When the wood finally and irrevocably caught, Diego was exhausted. He placed his sack beneath his head and curled up next to the fire and slept.

"You crazy Mexican!" Walking Dog shouted when he returned, nudging Diego with his boot. "It's not hot enough for you!"

Diego lost in his fiery dreams, grabbed a timber from the fire and shook it at Walking Dog. "Stay back!"

"Pedro, it's me. Walking Dog. Don't curse me with fire."

It took Diego moments to realize that it was, indeed, Walking Dog, not his stepfather, who lurked in his sleep.

"I am very tired," he said throwing the log into the fire.

"I can see that. Rest under the trailer out of the sun. You spook like some of my elders."

"Sorry."

"Don't be. We'll start the chili, then we'll both rest." Walking Dog rummaged in Bessie's interior and lugged out a cooler and an iron pot. They set to chopping meat, opening cans of beans, slicing onions and tomatoes and garlic.

Walking Dog browned the meat then added everything else. Diego sliced the narrow peppers, removed the seeds and added them to the pot, then he generously sprinkled spices into the chili.

"More chili powder. It masks my secret weapon," and Walking Dog held up a small red bottle of hot sauce. He uncapped the bottle and poured it into the mix. After carefully adjusting the fire and the pot, he said, "I'll feed and water Tonto, then we'll rest."

When their chores were done, they settled underneath the trailer.

"Walking Dog?" Diego asked sleepily.

"Yeah?"

"What if the hot sauce burns my throat?"

"Then I'll sing, and they'll shut the place down."

They slept soundly beneath the rusted trailer, shielded from the fierce sun, and woke to Hector's silver boots tapping the ground.

"The show's starting in an hour. Is supper ready? I can't go on on an empty stomach," he growled.

Diego and Walking Dog crawled out from beneath the trailer, their shirts stained with sweat.

"Dinner is served, *amigo*," and Walking Dog fetched three empty tin cans and some spoons.

Diego nudged the pot that simmered in the coals, and Walking Dog dished out the chili.

As they sat down to eat, Hector said, "I'm gonna impress them good ol' boys tonight. I'm banking on the gig at Dallas Rodeo Roundup next month."

Walking Dog coughed into his sleeve and wouldn't look at Diego. "I'm sure you'll get it."

"Have you heard me sing?" Hector asked Diego.

Diego shook his head.

"You know he sings too. Nice and smooth if you ever need a backup."

"Won't need it."

Mariachi music drifted slowly across the rodeo grounds, and it was sweet to Diego's ears. The sun began to falter and spread crimson across the sky. Walking Dog kicked dirt into the fire and drank deeply of the beer Hector shared. Lights came on around the grandstand.

"That's my cue," Hector said rising. "Thanks, boys for the grub. Here's the passes I promised. Good luck tomorrow," and he handed Walking Dog the tickets.

As they watched Hector waddle toward the grandstand,

Walking Dog said, "He won't make it to the first song. You ready?"

"*Sí.*"

"I can't wait to see his face when he asks you to stand in for him."

"We'll see."

They threw the cans into the car and hurried to the grandstand. The mariachi band was just winding down when they settled into their seats. Cowboys dressed in fine rodeo apparel rode horses with turquoise braided in their manes and tails. They paraded around the ring as a voice over the loudspeaker announced the opening of the rodeo.

"And for your listening pleasure, I am proud to introduce our time-honored friend, Hector Small." Hector appeared on a jury-rigged stage, took the microphone and croaked, "I am pleased to…" but his voice could go no further. He waved his arms to where Diego and Walking Dog were seated. "Excuse me. My voice, it seems, has taken a holiday. And he called, Walking Dog, your friend…" The crowd murmured.

"That's you," Walking Dog said as he nudged Diego. "That's your cue. Go on. Hurry now, before he changes his mind."

Diego walked down the stairs and nimbly leapt over the railing. Songs were spinning in his head. His throat felt tight. His breath was coming in short gasps. He had never seen so many people. As he trotted across the dusty ring, a great boom of applause sounded. When he climbed the steps to the stage, Hector growled in his ear.

"I'm gonna kill Walking Dog for this. You'd better sing pretty," he croaked and stomped off into the darkness.

The announcer held the mike to his mouth.

"And who do we have here?"

"Pedro Gómez." There was a small burst of laughter. Gnats streamed in the floodlight.

"And do you sing Pedro Gómez?"

"Like a sage sparrow," and Diego looked for Walking Dog, but the lights blinded him.

"Then sing," and the announcer handed him the mike and drew away into the darkness.

Diego took a moment, shuffling his feet, thinking of his father, wondering if he might be in the crowd. He cleared his throat and began to sing.

"*Si Adelita se fuera con otro la seguria por tierra y por mar…*" Diego sang for the first time in Spanish, and the crowd tittered, talked amongst themselves. If his father were in the crowd, he would know his Diego. He would know that only his son would sing La Adelita, a tribute to the women of the revolution, a song they had shared, and he had learned at his father's side when he was only five. He sang as if his heart would burst, and when he ended the song, the people were standing in the audience, and the sound they made was deafening.

He smiled at the faces he could not see.

"Take it easy. This is only the beginning," he whispered to himself. He began with the lullabies, his mother's story, then cowboy songs and finished with the "Yellow Rose of Texas."

"I thank you," he said to the audience before he took leave of the stage to thunderous applause.

As the announcer took the mike from Diego's hand, he shouted, "And that leads us to the prettiest flower in the state…Miss Penelope Johnson, our one and only sweetheart and rodeo queen."

Diego stumbled into the dark behind the stage. He knew he had never sung so well.

As he waited in the uncertain night, he thought vaguely of fire, wondered if embers still glowed at their campsite, wondered if a small, brown man might emerge, might claim him as his son.

He heard Miss Penelope talk of good works, talked of the events looming tomorrow. A girl bumped into him on her way to her seat. She was dressed in red calico, pop beads strung around her neck.

"Oh. Pedro? Pedro Gómez, was that you who just sang?"

"Yes," Diego said trying to get out of her way.

"You sing nice. My mother liked you, too, and she's hard to please."

"*Gracias.*"

"My father would like to meet you. He's a promoter. Music, you know."

"Yes," he said, watching the embers burn to a soft orange in his mind's eye, "but I am tired. Maybe tomorrow," and he walked away from her, away from the grandstand back to the trailer. Tonto whinnied and pranced in place as he approached. Walking Dog was right, he thought, there are many pretty *señoritas*. He kicked in the ashes, but the fire was dead.

The next morning they woke to clouds. Diego found a bucket and fetched water near the grandstand. The boys washed, ate the rest of the cold chili, and prepared for the calf roping event. Walking Dog insisted Diego braid his long black hair into a single plait and though Diego had seen his mother and sisters braiding hair, he fumbled the task so badly Walking Dog was forced to ask the assistance of Hector Small, who ambled up to their campsite.

"Not bad last night," he said handing Diego a ten dollar bill, "but it won't happen again. I sing tomorrow and forgo any dinner invitations," he said looking askance at Walking Dog. "Good luck today. After this, I'm off for the Fort Worth Stock Show and Rodeo. Hope your horse doesn't pick up any nails," and he sauntered off stopping here and there among the men.

"What does he mean?" Diego asked.

"He's a sore loser is all," Walking Dog said dismissively. "Get my lucky shirt. The red one. It's in the back seat."

Diego did as he asked, wondering at his luck. He had no luck. This he knew. Last night had been planned. He found the shirt and shaking it out asked Walking Dog, "Is there danger this calf roping?"

"Nah. Skill only and speed." Walking Dog put on the shirt, flipping his braid behind him, so it trailed down his back. "What do you think?"

"Lucky. Most lucky."

Diego brushed Tonto again, while Walking Dog saddled him. Deftly Walking Dog mounted him, and as if Tonto could sense the excitement, he began sidestepping, lowering his massive head and snorting. "Do you still have your pass?"

"*Sí.*"

"Those seats are good for the weekend. Get over there and see me ride," and with a halloo that woke the still sleeping cowboys, Walking Dog took off at a gallop toward the grandstand.

Diego grabbed his sack and made his way toward his seat through the gathering crowd.

A cowboy stuffed a pamphlet into his hand, but since he could not read he let it fall on the seat beside him. A tall, grizzled cowboy announced the calf roping event, and as one, and then another cowboy was led to the gate and a calf released, the flurry of rope flew, the calf lassoed around the neck, the cowboy jumping and then running and tying the calf in one swell swoop. He could not see Walking Dog mastering this. He was so easy, so languid in movement, that Diego could not see him doing this. Numbers were called out. Diego looked for Walking Dog and then finally spied him about three horses back. Tonto was pulling at the bit, jumping nervously.

"Next we have Pocohantas riding Tonto. Let's have a cheer for last year's winner," and the crowd broke into wild clapping and roars of good will. When the calf was released, it took only flying moments for Walking Dog to tie the calf. He stuck his hands into the air as if arrested, nodded to the judges and took Tonto's reins and led him out of the ring.

Diego hurried to the corrals behind the grandstand where he spotted Walking Dog leading Tonto back to the campsite.

"The numbers?"

"They were good, but not good enough. The third cowboy has the lead. I came in second."

Diego had wanted Walking Dog to win. He had been his friend, had shared his chili, and gave him the chance to sing. He

86

pulled from his sack the ten dollar bill.

"Here," he handed the bill to Walking Dog.

"What's this for?"

"For the ride. It took me a long way. It's for the ride." Diego thought to leave then. He did not want to be there tomorrow when the bull riding would take place when Walking Dog would lose again.

"It's a fortune. You're sure?"

"*Sí.*"

"Very well," and Walking Dog stuck it in his shirt pocket, stripped off his fancy red shirt, and laid it tenderly over the front seat in the car. "Well we're free for the day, and I've now got me ten bucks, let's feast."

Diego brushed the sweat from Tonto's withers, fed and watered him, and then they took off for the concessions. The clouds had been swept away with a strong, hot wind that kicked up the dried grass and dust.

"Last night a girl…" Diego began.

"I knew it. Can't trust a Mexican to not sweep up the girls," Walking Dog laughed.

"Not that. She say her father wants to meet me to sing."

"That's great. What did he say?"

"He did not say yet. I have to meet him."

"After the calf roping, everyone finds their way to food and drink. We'll find him."

"You are not sad?"

"For losing? Nah. It was not my day, but I'll stomp them in the bull riding."

"The bulls look mean."

"They are mean. The meaner, the better, for me. It's judged on man and beast. I'll be wanting a mean one."

That night they sat around their campfire while Walking Dog cooked mesquite and onion eggs. With full bellies and the next day looming, Walking Dog said, "Best get a good night's sleep. It's only eight seconds, but it takes a might of will. We'll take off after the bull riding. Load Tonto and off to the reservation. You'll like my people." Walking Dog's voice grew softer, "What are you doing out here?"

"I am seeing America."

"Sure. Good plan," and his voice trailed off.

They scrambled with their packs under the trailer and watched the stars until both boys were sleepy. Diego stretched out his sack for a pillow and dozed off. Hours later when the stars had shifted, he felt an arm across his shoulder, a hand clutched at his belly. He dreamed of his stepfather as the arm wore heavily on Diego's thoughts. Diego sweated as Walking Dog pressed up against him. He murmured in his sleep. He did not want to burn Walking Dog, did not even want to hurt his horse. He thought of the fire he would make with weathered barn planks, splinters flying as the fire grew strong. Crackling would fill the air. Diego waited until Walking Dog's breath subsided, his hand relaxed. As Walking Dog murmured, Diego was reminded of his stepfather after his rage and appetite had been spent when he would collapse over Diego and fondly whisper, *my dolly, my dolly*.

Diego knew in his heart it was not in Walking Dog's nature to injure, but his repulsion was great. He slipped out from under Walking Dog's brotherly arm and made his way silently, his sack in hand, through the battlefield of sleeping cowboys. He would not see Walking Dog ride the bull, would not see Tonto paw the ground as he had, in a wild beauty. He would not be there when Walking Dog won, not meet the girl's father who had promised a future. He wanted a fire, a strong, fierce blaze that would burn his demons, so he started walking north on the highway into the remote.

Chapter 9
A Small Brown Woman

He was open to the driver, the small brown woman who scolded him like his mother. He sat quietly as she warned him about the dangers of the road. Finally, to stop the barrage of words, he pleaded that he was searching for his father. She quieted.

He remembered the first time, before the beatings, before the beefy step-father had replaced his father. It was a time when it was just the two of them. His father carried a wooden box of refuse to the metal trash barrel. Diego watched as he splintered the box, and in remembering, it was as it always was, in slow motion. He placed the kindling in the barrel, heaped in paper sacks, cans emptied of their beans and tomato sauce, coffee grounds. The mess was dripping and bloody. He lit the edges of the paper sacks with Diamond Tip matches, held the match in the air until it fairly burned his fingers. Then as if in a trance, he blew them out and tossed them angrily into the fire that had caught. He picked up the stick, poked the fire a few times, asked Diego to stay put, to watch, and he left.

Diego remembered this because it was his sixth birthday. He watched the sparks and soot fly. He was mesmerized by the flames that licked the top of the barrel. As the fire waned, he pulled handfuls of grasses, Blue Grama, Bush Muhly and Buffalo Grass, running madly around the barrel, circling, going ever farther away to find fuel for the dying fire. He threw great armfuls of grass into the barrel, watching it smoke and steam, and finally flare.

When his father came around the corner of the house, he could have spoken sharply, but he did not. "Diego, slowly," he called softly. "Diego despacio, mas despacio." He stood next to Diego and said with reverence, "You have an inferno. Tienes un infierno." He placed his hands on Diego's shoulders and pulled him ever so slightly away from the fire, from the heat.

"Fire is beautiful but deadly in Texas. Fuego es precioso pero letal en Texas."

Diego was struck by his father's words, and in a perverse moment, everything had been altered. He swore he would never leave Texas, and though he had only just become six years old, he suddenly loved everything lethal.

"My Papa is a great singer," he lied more convincingly to her.

"You're lying," she said, looking nervously in the rearview mirror then jabbing Diego with her knuckles.

"My Papa."

"I said you're lying. No good Papa would have his son hitch-hiking all over, doing God knows what." She quickly crossed herself. "I don't wanna hear no more. When the storm is over, you can tell your stories to someone else."

It was true. The silence between them grew as stony as the splatter of raindrops on the windshield. She had slowed some. He dug in his sack for the map he had not checked since Abilene. He came up instead with a scrap of paper he had salvaged from a trash bin at the rodeo. It was a letter, smeared with chili sauce, barely legible from the brown water-soaked stain. He pressed it to his chest. He opened the paper, smoothed it on his lap.

"This is true. My Papa says to meet him in August. He will be singing at the Fort Worth Roundup and Rodeo." He folded the letter and slipped it back into his sack. "There. I will say no more about Papa."

The small, brown woman turned to look at him. The car

swerved with a gust of wind. The sky was a thick wall of grey.

After several miles, she asked, "And what does he sing?" as if the conversation had not been interrupted by the storm.

"Love. He sings love," Diego replied, pleased with the change in her attitude.

They lapsed into silence again until Diego rummaged in his sack and, like a rag picker, pulled out another piece of paper. It was a soiled bit of newspaper. He began to read, making up the words as he recited.

"Manuel Ramírez sung last night at the Prairie Run…"

"Don't. It makes me nervous. I believe you."

Diego folded the newsprint into a small square wedge and tucked it away in his sack.

"I would not lie about my Papa," Diego said, believing for the moment the words he spoke. The air in the car was thick and dense, the only sound the thwack thwack thwack of the windshield wipers. It was pouring, and Diego was grateful to this woman for believing and keeping him dry. The wind came up stronger pushing the car in sudden sweeps into the gravel at the edge of the road.

"Not much longer."

They drove over a bridge, the water roiling beneath them.

"Salt Fork River," she said bluntly, her knuckles white where she clenched the steering wheel. "We'll make for my place. Can't in good conscience drop you off in this."

Shortly she turned down a narrow dirt lane. A small, white house stood off in the distance. The lone tree bent in the wind.

"Oh my God," she said pulling up next to the house. It was then Diego saw it. Behind the grey wall of rain, a tornado circled dangerously near. She got out of the car and tugged at the basement door. She waved frantically to Diego, but he was frozen in his seat. She ran back to the car and screamed. "Get out! We need to get to cover! I need your help with the basement door!" When Diego did not respond, she ran around to his side of the car, wrenched the door open, and dragged Diego out into the rain. His fist tightened around his burlap sack. The rain and the howling wind brought Diego to his senses, and they rushed to the basement door. Diego pulled and pulled on the metal handle, and finally, it gave way. They hurried to shelter, and the storm rumbled as the door clanged shut.

The small brown woman swung around the cellar until she caught the string. When she pulled it, the room was full of ghastly white light that revealed dust and refuse. The woman retreated to a chair whose stuffing had erupted out of both arms. Diego stood lamely clutching his bag to his chest.

"Read to me," she said, her voice quavering. "Read that article about your father. I'd like to hear it now."

Diego crumpled onto the dusty floor. The wind whistled around them. There was an occasional thump as if a giant resided outside. He found the wad of paper, smoothed it, and began to read.

"Manuel Ramirez sang at the Prairie Hen Saloon last Friday night to a cheering crowd. His sweet voice filled the rafters as he sang of love. He will be appearing at the Forth Worth Roundup and Rodeo in August," Diego read. "It says more, but the paper is torn," and he tucked the paper into his pocket. "How long?" Diego asked sweeping his arm upward.

"Shouldn't be long. We'll know when it gets quiet," she paused, listening. "So your Papa is a singer. Does he make good money?"

"Some."

"Does he send it to your Mama?"

"He does," Diego stammered, his eyes suddenly welling with tears more for his lies than his mother.

The small brown woman pulled a tattered blanket over her legs, closed her eyes, and breathed deeply.

"Why is it then that you travel north with me rather than head south to Fort Worth?"

"I have adventure."

"Some adventure," she laughed opening her eyes. "I don't have children," she rose then trailing the blanket with her, "but if I did, I certainly wouldn't let them wander God knows where with God knows who."

She did not know who Diego had left behind. She did not know about the fire, or his sisters, or his stepfather. She knew only what Diego had told her, and he was suddenly angry with her for all she implied.

There was a time that came when he forgot when the beatings began. He wondered if he had somehow started it, had forgotten to water the horses or left a saddle in the rain. He came to an understanding with the heavy, sweating hulk that collapsed on him two or three times a week. He had tried to avoid him, would pretend not to listen, but this angered him more. The beatings would become swift and brutal and finally, exhausted, Diego fell in with the erratic rhythms. Like the twister outside, he grew a skin sensible to the wind.

Like teeth chattering the cellar door lifted and closed. Diego looked at the woman. *Perhaps she is praying*, he thought. He thought he might comfort her, but as he thought, he heard a mighty clunk on the side of the house. Glass shattered somewhere overhead. He thought of his lies, and they were good.

Diego lost track of time. Heading east the wind howled like a runaway train. The woman stood beneath the small, lone window.

"It's easing," she whispered. "Heading east." She walked to the unfinished stairway, put her hand on the railing. "You coming?" and she stepped onto the narrow treads and made her way to the kitchen. Diego followed trailing his sack across the dirt floor.

The kitchen was precise, small and clean, the counters empty of cups and spoons, canisters, or dishrags. His own mother's kitchen was a medley of smells, spices, pork fat, plates unwashed, and opened cans. His mother would feel unwelcome here, shut out. He had not thought of his mother for days. She would know he had taken her coins, her life savings. She would know he had taken her man as she called his stepfather, would know that he had burned in Diego's flames. She would know that neither of them, his stepfather, or he, would be coming back. She would have to bury his stepfather alone without her pennies. His sisters would look on and cry. He had done this. He felt no remorse. She had, after all, not rescued him. The walls were thin. She had not thrust open the door and exposed the brute for what he was. Diego was hungry. He waited for the small, brown woman to ask him if he would eat as he knew she would. She had, after all, saved his life.

"I don't want to look out just yet," she said, closing the faded yellow curtains. She opened the refrigerator and took out a jar of grape jelly. "In there you'll find a loaf of bread."

Diego opened the door to a small pantry. Cans of vegetables, potted meats, jars of homemade tomato sauce filled the shelves. On a narrow counter, he found the bread, the bread was light and white, not like his mother's dark brown loaves. He carried it to the woman. A foil package of soft white cheese lay on the counter, and she spread the bread with cheese and jelly.

Gathering two plates, she laid the sandwiches on them and placed them on the square brown table. "Sit. Eat."

Diego wanted to leave. The storm was over. It had left no destruction. He was itchy to be back on the road.

"I will take this and go," he said fingering the plate.

Suddenly she was no longer small, but, instead, a big black cloud towering over him.

"I said sit. Eat." her voice steely. "You want milk?"

"*Sí, gracias.*"

She poured the milk into glasses and brought them to the table. Her breath rattled as she sat.

"It is no good pretending this did not happen."

"*Sí,*" Diego replied, not understanding.

"The ride, so innocent, the rain, the wind, the twister." She shook her head. "I don't want to look outside."

"It has passed. It is safe." Diego rose and pulled the curtains apart. "Your tree, the beautiful one beside the house, has no more leaves. There is a cart overturned and tumbleweeds, but nothing dead from it. It passes." He stood behind her, the dark cloud surrounding her gone.

He wanted to embrace her as he had embraced his mother. His eyes watered, and he brusquely swept them away with his sleeve. She had saved him, had jarred him from his frightened stillness in the car. Though he had almost forgotten Ralph Preston, he would not forget her. He took the glass of milk and drank it. He reached for the sandwich, and she put her hand on his.

"Be safe."

"*Gracias, señora,*" and he took the sandwich and left her alone in the dim kitchen.

Chapter 10:
Water

The sun pricked the grey sky, letting in hazy, amber light. It was mid-afternoon. He wondered how many days had passed. His shoes slapped against the road, his soles thin. *Many days*, he thought. There was a rainbow hue, the browns of grains and grasses, mostly burned out, dried, but a rainbow all the same. His nose itched with the heat, the dried chaff on the leftover wind. He walked back along the way he had come past refuse left by the twister, past the small houses, and back to the Salt Fork, the river they had crossed before the storm. The sun was low in the sky when he finally reached the river.

A stand of trees along the near bank, far from the bridge and houses, far from the thoughts of drivers who picked up stray boys, provided him shelter. He stripped off his clothes and waded into the water. His scars burned with dried sweat. He took the clothes he wore and the spare he carried in his sack and scrubbed them against the rocks. He splashed in the sluggish water then hung his clothes to dry on the bushes that surrounded him. He was hungry and opened his last can of beans, scooping the rich, dark mass into his mouth. He washed again and wondered how he had taken cleanliness for granted.

He wanted to be busy before dark fell. He was uneasy about sleeping outdoors. The ranch had taught him about the dangers, snakes and insects, so he cleared a patch of brush to sleep upon. He took stock of his belongings, dumping them in the clearing. He had his can opener, his mother's coins, his Fanta bottle and the limp dollars he had earned at the saloon. Fourteen dollars, more money than he had ever seen. The yellow book the burning man had given him, the dented pot, the map and the papers he had hidden in his sack along the way, he coveted. He shook out the wrinkled map and thought, Lubbock, a city, *a place where he could earn more,* refolded it and stuck it into the sack along with everything except his papers. He would read some before the light fell.

A small, waxy paper, a butter wrapper had markings, and he could make them out. 1 cup, ½ cup, ¼ cup. Dairy Pride Butter, salted. He could make out these words, and it filled him as he hurried on to another paper. The next paper was torn. Room $15/wk, well-ligh… Scraps he had pilfered from the brush began to fall around him and suddenly he was at the end, except for the yellow book. He did not want to think of the man, the tumbleweeds, the gasoline, the books, the recipe for fire. He no longer had his matches, his precious Diamond Tips, the sticks worn and silky, but he built a fire anyway even if he could not light it. He did not want the dark to come, he thought as he sat naked on the bank. He put the yellow book and his other things back into his sack. He walked again to the water, drank deeply, filled his bottle, and set about gathering kindling.

He built a small castle of sticks, a fortress, stuffed papers he had read into the center and covered them with small bits of brush. He did not want to think of the small, brown woman, her hand jerking his arm, leading him to safety. He did not want to think of her kindness. He tried to be brave beside a fire he could not light, but his hands shook. As the light fell, his guardian angel prayer spoken, he kicked the sticks asunder.

Except for his clothes, he gathered his sack and made a pillow. He stared at the starless sky. He listened to the rustlings of night creatures. He spoke again his guardian angel prayer and finally fell into sleep.

There were times when his stepfather was filled with remorse. "My Dolly," he'd cry, thick-tongued as he lay against Diego, sweating and smelling of onions and garlic. "I come from Mexico. I speak only English, no Spanish, to get along, to get along with the bosses. I lie on grass nights. It is no how it seems," and he put his thumb on the back of Diego's neck. "I pick tomatoes, peppers. I pick oranges. I pick anything," his voice becoming oily. "Blood and blisters. Then I come here to your Mama. Pretty. Widowed. I take you in, gave your Mama money. I work for you. It is no how it seems," then he slapped Diego's back, "This," he said his voice tight and angry, "This is nothing." He pulled the covers over Diego's legs, and he pulled on his pants. As he left the room, at the door, he called softly as if this had not happened, "Dolly, time to water the horses."

Diego woke with a shudder. He smelled garlic and onions, his stepfather's sweat. He breathed uneasily. The water bubbled quietly in the river. His fire sticks lay scattered at his feet. He was without matches. He shuddered.

Chapter 11:
The Farm

The morning brought a great inverted bowl of heat. Diego was weary from his dreams. He slipped into the cool water of the Salt Fork, soaked his head and clumsily washed his hair.

It had grown long, and he straightened it with his fingers. He pulled on Millie's shirt and overalls, which were still damp along the seams. He took his old clothes and tied them securely around his mother's coins, stuffed them into the bottom of his bag, and carefully repacked, placing his dollars in the pocket of his old pants.

The rides had left him ragged, remembering, conjuring, scared. He walked on the wrong side of the road and let the oncoming traffic wash over him. His stomach growled. He checked his map. Spur was only a few miles up the road. He could purchase a cold drink, beans, matches. He would pay. He was in the wild country, traffic was sparse, he couldn't afford to get caught stealing. He was wary and proud of his craftiness.

He heard it long before he felt the motor's vibration behind him. He didn't turn to look back. It was large and moving slowly. Suddenly it was beside him, a large red tractor etched with use. The man driving was mowing the wild grass alongside the road.

"It don't look like much," the man called to Diego, "but it beats walking in this heat." The man wore a straw hat, sweat ran in rivulets down his weatherbeaten and wrinkled face. "Step up on the hitch behind me and hold onto the seat. It swivels some so take a good hold."

Diego hesitated. He stood on the other side of the road, his bag dragging. The man took no notion of moving. He sat there, wiped the sweat on his face on his faded blue shirt. "I can wait here all day." He set the idle lower. "Ain't like I have a lot to do 'til my cotton comes in. Come on. It's too hot to be ornery."

Diego lifted his arm and started across the road.

"Just up behind here. It's wide enough for you and your stuff."

"*Gracias*," and Diego picked his way until he was standing behind the man. He could smell ivory soap and sweat.

"I'm going to start her up. She bucks some. Hold on."

The tractor roared into life and drowned out any ordinary conversation.

The mower blade sliced through the thick weeds that grew alongside the road. The air was full of dried plant dust.

The man shouted, "Making a fire break. First spark of a lit cigarette, and this will all go up in smoke. God knows we could use some rain," then he turned back to his work cajoling the tractor slightly to the left and then slightly to the right. "My cotton's come in," he shouted again. "Don't need no fire."

Diego stiffened. The man was old. What did he know of fire?

"Pearson Radford," he slung his arm back to take Diego's hand.

"Pedro, Pedro Gómez," Diego replied placing his sweaty hand in the old man's.

"You looking for work?"

"*Sí.*"

"My farm's just up from here. Got a barn I need to paint. You paint?"

"*Sí,*" he shouted in the old man's ear.

"Elmer can't do it no more. Can't climb, but he's good on the jinny."

"Jinny?"

"For picking the cotton. Elmer's a good jinny man."

They were closing up on a long, narrow dirt lane. Every spare spot of prairie was taken up with cotton. Green and a few feet tall, it seemed to Diego that it might survive the drought.

"They've cut back on the irrigation, but I think it will hold."

A white, two-story house sat in a clearing, Pearson parked the tractor next to a barn scarred with weather. Diego climbed down. He felt dizzy from the dust and hunger. His legs wobbled.

The man started toward the house, then turned back.

"You want to start work now or feed your face?" and the old man smiled, showing a mouth full of straight teeth. The corners of his mouth sat in a fixed grin.

"Face," Diego laughed.

"Good. I don't trust a man, who don't trust his stomach," and he slapped Diego on the back. "You'll meet the Missus. Don't mind her. She's a fuss buzzard but the best-darned cook."

The ground was scorched to bare, dry earth, and they kicked up dust as they made their way to the house. As they entered through the kitchen door, a black man, tall, wiry, sat at a long wooden table.

"Ya found someone to paint the barn?"

"Pedro meet Elmer. I was telling him you just about the best jinny man these parts."

"I am. I am. Youse a skinny one and small. Bet you climb a ladder like a monkey," he said taking Diego in. "Come. Set, before I eat all them biscuits."

"Where can I wash?" Diego said holding out his hands.

Pearson nodded toward the sink where a short, plump woman stood at the stove stirring chicken and gravy.

"Don't eat all those biscuits Elmer or they'll be nothing to put the gravy on," she nodded to Diego as if strangers in her kitchen were an everyday occurrence. As Diego washed, Pearson came up behind him.

"Don't let it run long. We're short on water."

Diego dried his hands on a towel the woman handed him and took the seat Elmer pointed out to him.

"You from Spur?" Elmer asked, handing him the platter of hot biscuits.

"No."

"From where then?" the woman asked, taking a seat at the end of the table.

"El Paso."

"Whooee!" Elmer whistled. "You a long way from home."

"He's here now. Suits me," Pearson muttered, soaking his biscuits with chicken and gravy.

"Suits you to have that barn painted no matter what?"

"Pardon me. I got to sit out the growing season somehow," he said nodding to his wife. "This is Effie Radford. My one and only. Take more gravy, Pedro. It ain't chicken and gravy elsewise."

They quarreled easily throughout the meal. Effie railed one minute and laughed the next. Elmer ate noisily, and Diego furiously devoured everything put in front of him. Effie rose to fetch a pot of rich, dark coffee, set it down on the table and began to clear the plates. She paused before Diego.

"Can I get you something more?"

"No. *Gracias*."

"Well, then. I'll fetch some linens. You'll sleep out in the bunkhouse with Elmer," and she disappeared into the recesses of the house. Diego listened to her footsteps as she made her way upstairs.

"She's a mother hen when it come to visitors," Pearson said. "Mind she don't talk your ear off. I got a barn to paint."

"No, Sir."

"Name's Pearson. Folks call me Pearse."

"Pearse."

"Can't wait to see this monkey climb," Elmer said emptying his cup.

"Best get started," Pearson said rising. "Elmer, show Pedro the paint and the brushes. Have him start on the shady side. The heat's fierce."

Elmer nodded, and Pedro and Elmer started out the door. Pearson called after them.

"Waited ten years to paint this barn. Take your time."

Elmer walked Diego into the bunkhouse, a small, low, barn-like structure, with six wooden bunks, a wash basin, and bench. Elmer pulled the string on the bare light bulb, and the room was awash in dust motes.

"Home. At least as long as the barn needs paint. Pick your bunk."

Diego chose a bed under the window and stowed his bag under the pillow.

"Got running water if you wants it. Outhouse is around the back. All the comforts of home," Elmer chuckled, lying down on his bed. "Got to gets some things straight. I's the foreman, the jinny man. I sees the crop start. I sees to the finish. All the rest that lays in between is my time. Like I say, I's the foreman, even if the fore ain't but you and me. Don't be gettin' notions. You do as I say, you'll get along. Speak English, while you're here. Save your *gracias* for the *señoritas*."

"*Sí*," Diego stammered. "Yes."

"You'll do," Elmer said, looking him over. "You'll do just fine." He rose. "Git yourself settled, then meet me in the barn."

"Yes."

The bunkhouse was hotter than staring into the sun. He washed his face under the faucet, the Salt Fork River only a memory. It's how it is, Diego thought. Starts and stops, faces, lives in between, moving like the picture shows he had never seen.

Effie interrupted his daydreaming. Her hands were full of sheets, a well-washed towel, and a cotton blanket.

"Where are you bunking?" Diego pointed. Hurriedly he removed his bag and put it on the floor.

"I can do that," he said, taking the bundle from her, setting it on the bed next to his. He stood there, and suddenly she took up the sheets and with a quick crack split the bundle open and laid it on the bed. Diego laughed.

Laughing too, she said, "I've done this a lot."

Together they spread the sheets, the blanket and while she was stuffing the pillow into its case, she said, "After supper, I'll get you a pencil and paper. Best you let your Ma and Pa know where you are. I'll post it tomorrow."

Diego didn't know what to say. He could no longer imagine the ranch, the small house, his mother, his sisters. He had not thought to write them.

"*Gracias*," but I have it here," and he tapped the pocket on his chest where his map lay. The paper crackled. "I'll write and send it when I get to Spur."

"You'll be a week at least painting that barn. I'm going into Spur tomorrow. I'll post it for you." She backed away then, surveyed their handiwork and said, "I hope you'll be comfortable."

"*Gracias*. The chicken gravy was good."

"You think so. Always think it needs a pinch more salt," and she winked and left Diego, the dust motes fiery in the sunlight.

He hurried into the barn. Elmer was already there, a paint can in each hand, making a wide swinging arc.

"Shake 'em up good 'fore you open them. Paint's been sitting for three years."

Diego grabbed a can and mimicked Elmer. Chickens scratched in the straw-covered, earthen floor. He remembered a time, a night when he could have wrung a chicken's neck in the shed in Odessa. It seemed long ago. The chickens gave them a wide berth. Elmer set his cans down.

"Wipe 'em clean fore you open them. Paintbrush's there," and he pointed to a pair of saw horses. A plank sat on top.

"When you finish, clean the brush good. Gasoline's there," and he pointed to a grease-smeared can by the door. "Ya got all that?"

"*Sí.*"

"I said did you get all that?" he said irritably.

"Yes."

"Good. Shake each about five minutes, stir 'em up some with a stick. Ladder's all set," and Elmer left.

Diego's arms were tiring already, and he had six more cans to go. The chickens closed in seeing he wasn't any danger.

Mama asked him to kill a chicken. Diego's mouth had watered thinking about chicken. He had gone into the yard where the hens were digging in the dust, talking among themselves. He picked one out, a white hen, who sat at the corner of the house preening. He crept slowly, and as he neared his prey, the hen shot off. He chased after it, running around the yard, scattering hens left and right. Finally, as the hen was trapped against the house, Diego caught her up in his arms. The hen wriggled, her feathers tickling Diego's nose, making Diego laugh. He stretched the hen out between his two hands and succeeded in holding her in one. The hen's neck strained against her captor, but Diego could not snap its neck. His fist wouldn't close. His fingers danced against the hens feathers and then fled. He tried again and again. Tears had streamed down along his cheeks. His mother came to the door. She watched him struggle with himself. Her lips trembled with mirth until she was laughing loud and uncontrollably.

"Diego. Here," she said, taking the squirming chicken from his hands. With one deft movement, the chicken was lifeless. "Diego, we must feast on your birthday, no?" she said still laughing. Diego had turned seven, his stepfather only a future nightmare.

Diego swung another set of cans. He did not know what to think. The thought that his mother could kill so easily haunted him. He wondered from where the memory had sprung. Perhaps it was the morning breakfast, he thought, trying to reassure himself. The afternoon continued, haunted with memories. While he climbed the ladder, paint can and brush in tow, he thought he heard the high, frightened whinnying of horses. While he brushed the white paint into the dry, weathered boards, he saw their wide, bulging eyes. He teetered on the ladder's rung until the visions passed, lathering paint, wiping sweat from his brow, descending, moving the ladder, climbing again. The chickens gathered at the base of the ladder, clucking and scratching as if they knew he was a coward, but he continued to paint until late into the afternoon. The paint was sucked into the wood like a thirsty man. He painted over and over in one spot until the boards were quenched. The chickens whispered among themselves. He thought he might fall.

"Don't have a stroke on us," a voice called. It seemed like it came from far away. He looked down, and it was as if the earth, were in motion. His legs felt wobbly. The voice came again. "You missed lunch. Must be hot and thirsty. There's a pitcher of cold water in the frig. Glasses are on the drain board." A woman, the farmer's wife, Diego recognized, was carrying a basket of eggs. "Anytime you need a drink. Drink." Diego waved and called his thanks. He watched her as she walked into the house. He had finished painting the top half of the side of the barn. He climbed down slowly, his hands clutching the sides of the metal ladder and closed the lid of the paint can. The sun hung in the west.

He set the paintbrush on the sawhorse table in the barn, found a rag, and wiped his hands. He discovered an old can, poured the gasoline, and set the paintbrush to soak. He crossed the yard to the house. His lips were dry, and his tongue felt thick. He crossed the narrow porch and knocked at the kitchen door. He waited for what seemed like days. He tried the handle. The door gave, and he entered cautiously.

"Hello. Mrs. Radford?"

The house was silent. Not able to contain his thirst, he opened the refrigerator door. Taking a glass from the drain board, he filled it. He emptied glass after glass. He shivered, his sweat cooling. A coffeepot simmered on the stove. He listened carefully, but the house remained quiet. He opened a drawer along the kitchen counter. It was full of coins, twine, papers, screws and nuts and bolts. A pack of matches was wedged under a nail file. He pulled the matches free and placed them on the counter. Water sloshed in his belly.

"If you're gonna smoke. Do it on the porch. It's a tinder box out there," Effie said disapprovingly behind him.

Diego, immediately alert, pushed the drawer shut and closed his palm over the matches. "Spoon?" he managed.

"Spoon?"

"For coffee. May I?"

"Of course. I should have told you," she said, entering the kitchen, pulling a cup from where it had been drying. She poured Diego a cup of coffee and one for herself.

"Do you have your letter?"

"I lose," he said, patting his chest pocket. "I lose painting."

"Never mind. You can write one tonight after supper. Which reminds me I'd better get started or we'll be eating rice and beans."

Diego finished his coffee in silence, rose, took his cup to the sink.

"Dinner will be in about an hour."

He passed Pearson on his way to the bunkhouse.

"Side looks good. Soaking up a lot of paint though. Think I'll drive into Spur with Effie tomorrow. Pick up a couple more gallons." He tipped his straw hat at Diego. "See you at supper."

In the bunkhouse, Diego stripped to the waist. He soaked his head under the cold tap. He washed his face and scrubbed underneath his arms. He was happy. He would have a full belly soon. He sat on his bunk and struck the paper sticks, *not as good as my Diamond Tips,* he thought. He watched them flare, blue, orange, and let them die, scorching his fingertips. He heard Elmer struggling with drink outside. Hurriedly, he gathered the spent matches and hummed a Texas song when Elmer stumbled in.

"Thought I'd hear a song from you boy. Something like a bird. Something like "Amazing Grace! How sweet the sound. That saved a wretch like me," and he began to sing, a deep, dark baritone and though Diego didn't know the words, the melody was familiar, and he began to hum. "You got a nice thrum, but you should heed the words, the words is powerful. Get a shirt on, supper's bein' served."

Elmer was clearly drunk. Diego had seen drunk before. But as the two of them made their way across the spit of grass that separated the bunkhouse from the house, Elmer stood up straight like a post was set against his back and walked into the house as sober as an undertaker.

"I smelled smoke in that bunkhouse. Missus say all fire be done on the porch. Y'all burn us down otherways. There's a kettle on the porch for smokin'."

Effie stood at the stove. Pearse sat at the head of the table. Diego and Elmer sat across from each other. The smells that wafted around the kitchen almost made Diego faint. Effie came around each of them and heaped pot roast and potatoes, carrots in gravy on each plate. A basket of bread stood on the table. A tall glass of milk stood at Diego's elbow, and it took all his concentration not to down it in one gulp.

"I was telling Pedro, the barn looks good. You're a good worker, son. I appreciate that. There's no telling how a man will show himself. You done good," and he lifted his glass of milk and downed it in one gulp. "Elmer? How's the jinny?"

"Oiled and tweaked and ready to go."

"The weather's talking rain Friday," Effie added.

"The west field is drying up. We could certainly use some."

Diego could not follow their conversation. He focused on the steaming plate before him. He had never seen so much food whose scent was heavenly. He waited, silent, for grace. When it gratefully came and went, he took up his fork with a bit of potato, a bit of meat and carrot and scooped it into his mouth. *This is a good place*, he thought. He determined to slow his painting, to enjoy the good food, a place to sleep and wash. He would be a good worker, Pearse was proud, he had said so. Maybe there would be other jobs.

"Pedro, how'd you come up from El Paso?" Pearse asked.

Diego set his fork on his plate and waited for a lie to take shape. So mesmerized by the dinner, he could not form one.

"Odessa, Midland, Sweetwater, then Abilene, then north."

"That's a long way for a boy," Effie said, spooning another serving onto Diego's plate.

"He ain't a boy. Why you're seventeen, eighteen? Am I right?"

"Eighteen."

"What made you leave home?" Elmer asked.

"My stepfather died," and Diego choked, spluttering and coughing.

"Had to pay the bills. Know how it is. Thought my boys would stay on the farm. We grew sugarcane then. A bad crop this far north. But they left. One became a salesman, the other an itinerant. Does most anything, but can't set his mind on a place. Somewhat like you, Pedro. Leastways you can hold a brush steady."

"Pearse, ya workin' this boy too hard. Gonna eat you out of home."

"Boy's earned it. Elmer the roof needs tending. Next squall will have the barn awash. Pedro, can you handle roof work?"

"I can handle the roof."

"Good. When the barn's finished, Elmer will show you where the tarpaper, tar, and nails are. Elmer, what you say we up his pay a dollar?"

"Suits me," Elmer muttered into his plate.

"You send money to your mother?" Effie asked Diego.

"*Sí.*" Elmer glared at him. "Yes."

"You can't make much being always on the road."

"I sing. Make good money."

"Leave the boy to his meal, Effie. He can hold up his head. That's enough for me, Elmer."

They finished the meal in satisfied silence.

"Pedro. I made a cake to celebrate your first day of work with us. First, you write your letter. I'll put a stamp on it and post it tomorrow."

"I lost it," he said. "I lost it painting I think."

"Never mind. I have paper. Come with me. You can write another." He reluctantly followed her into the living room. A desk stood under the window. Large stuffed chairs sat on either side of a low wooden table. Seed catalogs were piled high on either side of the chairs. She went to the desk and pulled a piece of paper from the drawer and gave him a pencil.

Except for some simple words, Diego could neither read Spanish nor write much English. Clumsily he held the pencil over the blank page writing in English to spite his mother. She would have to ask a ranch hand to interpret. Diego had not forgotten, the thin walls, his cries, and the door forever closed.

Mama
I am shame to fire barn. I am far El Paso. I work. Paint barn. Sing. I OK. I miss. I send more.
Diego

He folded the paper and slipped in two dollar bills. Effie handed him an envelope, and Diego sealed it. He dictated his mother's name and the ranch address to Effie who wrote it in a delicate scrawl across the envelope.

"Your mother will be pleased, Pedro. She must be worried silly."

When he was five, he lit his first fire. It was a small thing, grasses caught, thistles, a fence, a small thing. He went far away from that paltry fire. Little fires, little fires that spent themselves. He smelled like smoke and Constantina, his mother, scrubbed it away after his father left, and after his stepfather had come to stay.

Diego left her, walked through the kitchen and out onto the porch. Elmer rocked slowly on the settee. Diego started across the spare grass.

"Where ya goin'? There's cake and coffee still. Want to catch up on your singin'?"

Diego motioned to the outhouse and walked on. His words haunted him. *I am shame to fire barn. Was killing a stepfather cause for shame?* He did not know. He had had to run. There were so many times he could not explain, times when his stepfather tired of him.

When Esmerelda stood on tiptoe to put the dinner plates away, his stepfather's black eyes followed the muscles in her back, her hips, her legs. He shoved his cup across the table and winked at Diego, and Diego's supper would churn in his belly. He shouted at Esmerelda to take the garbage to the trash barrel, a job that was usually his. Diego wanted to run and felt the thin wings of fear creep up on him. His fingers drummed on the table-top until his stepfather slapped his hand on his. Esmerelda turned angrily about to scold him for his laziness, but she stopped. Their stepfather was glaring at her. Diego couldn't meet her gaze.

Diego sat in the outhouse and felt for his matches. He had burned them carelessly. He would have to conserve. Diego's body was healing, the scars fading. Hope, an invalid thing, crept up on him. He thought of his sisters and worried his stepfather was still alive. He did not join them for coffee and cake. He did not sing.

Days passed, the sun burned his skin, but, at last, the barn was painted. Nights he spent alone in the bunkhouse, learning new songs. Effie had lent them a radio. That night, after the brushes were cleaned, the paint cans hauled to the garbage heap, the ladder stowed again in the barn, Elmer strolled into the bunkhouse. El-mer sat back on the back of his bunk, his hands clasped behind his head while Diego practiced the songs.

"Pedro. Pedro," he crooned. "Be singin', so I suppose you are happy here? *Sí?*"

Diego nodded.

"In my years I seen many men come and goin'. I can smell it like dust. Either they be runnin' to or runnin' from. I 'pect you be the kind that runs from," Elmer waited, but Diego remained silent. "I's climbed the backs of many men. Mucho. Men better'n you. The missus likes you, and Pearse respects you, but there's only room for one foreman," Elmer stood. "I won't be put to pasture. Do what Pearse say and climb up that ladder. Fix them holes, tar them shut, but when the crop come in, about a week or two now, you 'member I's the jinny man. No song's gonna wash you clean in my eye. No mind what Pearse say, you keep on runnin'. You hear me good or else that runnin' gonna catch. You get me?"

"*Sí.*"

"Go on. Sing your heart out," and Elmer sauntered just as slowly as his words had out of the bunkhouse.

Diego hauled tarpaper and tar and brushes and nails up onto the roof. It was a cloudy, humid day, and the cotton speckled the land. Diego had avoided Elmer since that night, and his songs grew heavy and sad, but here he was on top of the world, and he thought of his Papa. He was proud to work, and as he lifted the rotten tarpaper with a pry bar, he thought how his father would have been at home here. How such peaceful thoughts were so easily replaced by reliving nightmares frightened him. They were becoming more frequent, and his steady hand trembled, his feet uneasy on the dry roof. He did not know when his next fire would be or where.

After a beating, he set little fires when he could get away out in the prairies, hidden by the curves of hills, ravines, little fires that set the cattle to lowing. When he returned, he began to follow his stepfather, mocking his swagger and short-limbed stride, and the cowboys laughed.

He worked tirelessly, skipping the midday meal, hungrily devouring supper in silence.

"You're gonna wear yourself down to bone," Pearse chided.

Other days Effie called him down from the roof with a parcel of lunch and a tumbler of water.

Diego felt powerful on the roof. No one could touch him. Nights, on the porch, he sang for Pearse and the Missus remembering that his father was not God, could not sing, had broken his word to his family, and had forsaken him. Standing on the roof in his flapping shoes, he sang at the top of his lungs as he knelt with hammer and nail, so loud that Pearse and Elmer emerged from the barn and the Missus came to the porch, her hand shielding her eyes to hear him sing.

As the roof neared completion, Elmer dogged him so that Diego was never alone with Pearse. Diego was not angry with Elmer. He did not feel guilt. He had paid and repaid his stepfather's brutality. When he had seen him enter the burning barn, he had felt the joy that came with fire. He knew he had to leave. He had told them of Millie's kindness and Walking Dog's friendship. He had told of the tornado and the cream cheese and jelly sandwich from the small, brown woman. As he spoke haltingly of his travels, he felt unfinished, a sadness, and he knew he would feel the same way when he left the cotton farm. He had been changed by his travels, and it felt like a pair of shoes that didn't fit.

The work was done. There was only the jinny, and he was not the foreman. He washed his paint-spattered clothes in the basin, hung them to dry. He was leaving. He knew this. He would miss Pearse's praise and Effie's suppers. Elmer had grown stiff, and bitter, and spoke to him rarely. He slipped up behind Diego, holding him fast by the shoulders when Pearse talked of the crop, his plans. There would be no more work, no painting or joyous moments on the roof. He had only to form his goodbye, his tongue thickening with English words, tears smarting at the corners of his eyes.

When Pearse cornered him with work for another week until the crop came in, Diego refused, said he had business in Lubbock. Effie made a bundle of sandwiches and asked him how they could contact him if his mother sent a letter. Lubbock, General Delivery. As Diego walked the long, narrow lane to the road, Elmer stood square in the grassy place between the barn and the house and stared after him. Elmer called out when Diego reached the road.

"No hard feelings!"

Without turning, his eyes swollen with tears, Diego called back. "Not hard."

Chapter 12:
Girl

He thought she was a mirage, a speck, a wall of water along-side the road that waved and shimmered. He hastened his step, his shoes flapping and catching in the dirt, though he had tied them with twine. He had walked far from the cotton farm, and though cars and beat up trucks passed him, he neither waved nor flagged them. He hurried, hot and stumbling, willing himself to chase his dream. Soon she appeared, no longer a ghost. He could discern her wide back and then the long, black braid that swung at her waist. He was reminded of his mother. He wanted to call out in greeting but feared she might disappear. The distance between them grew shorter, and she turned at the slap slap his shoes made on the road. She stooped and thrust something into a bag she carried over her shoulder, turning once again to her work.

Diego suddenly saw she was picking up stray bottles and scrambled in the grass until he found an empty glass bottle.

"Hey," he called, sweating and out of breath, and he held the bottle in the air.

She stopped and hesitantly walked a few steps in Diego's direction. "Hello," she called.

"*Hola,*" Diego replied, and Diego cut the distance between them until he was standing close enough to smell her dry grassy scent. He hesitated. She was beautiful with a wide face and delicate chin, her brown skin gleaming with sweat. "Diego Ramírez," he said bravely, wondering if she read the newspapers, wondering if his name had been linked to fire.

"Rosalia López," she said, smiling shyly.

"I see you get bottles."

"*Sí.* The store gives money."

"I am walking, too. I'll help."

She was unsure and looked around her on the empty road. "I'll look myself."

Diego, too, looked at the empty road as if he had come home. "*Hablas Español?*" he asked.

"You speak good English. Speak English. I will become beauty girl, cut hair, make fashion. Must speak good."

"Where?"

"A few miles. Lubbock. There is salon."

"I paint and fix roofs," he said proudly. "Not far. I go to Lubbock, too. Singer," and he hummed a few lines.

They started walking. Her bag rattled with glass.

"They throw them to side," she said hoisting her bag. "Here," she said, running into the prairie, "and here," she said, stooping to pick up another bottle. As she knelt, the glass in the bag made a crashing noise.

"You will have only dust. I'll look." Diego said, scurrying off into the brush that lined the road.

"Here and here!" he cried, holding up two empty bottles. "And more. Plenty!"

He ran back to her and gently dropped the glass into the bag. He stayed at her side until she pointed into the prairie, and Diego disappeared where the grass grew high, and worried, she cried out.

"Diego Ramírez, do not tease."

Diego's head popped out of the weeds and held up his hands. "Four!"

He welcomed the heat and the sweat. He was not hitchhiking now. His arm was not thrust out to seek a new town, to hear a driver's story. He was walking with a pretty girl, and he was giddy. When he was not scrambling in the grass, he walked close, her skirt brushing against his leg. He wanted to take her hand, to look in her brown steady eyes.

"Where are you going?" she asked suddenly.

"To Lubbock. Don't know. That's true. I don't know."

"Cars pick you up?"

"Yes, many drivers since El Paso."

"Is where you from?"

"Yes."

She shrugged. "You go in cars with no purpose. That's not smart. I am going home now. This sack grows heavy." She lifted the sack and rubbed her shoulder. "I should hear you sing? Lubbock, no?" She smiled and turned down a small dirt lane. Diego followed. "No. My Mama would not like boys to help." And she stood there waiting for Diego to leave.

Diego, at once, wanted to strike and embrace her. He waited for her to leave. When she finally left him gazing after her, he whispered her name, Rosalia López, committing the lane, the highway, her broad back to memory. He would be back. He would sing in Lubbock. She would come. Perhaps they would kiss.

He sat down on the side of the lane, opened his sack, and took out his map. Two miles from Spar, he thought, two miles.

Chapter 13:
Sheriff

Diego remembered the feel of her skirt against his leg. He stopped and stopped again, looking for landmarks, anything to mark the place so he could return. Rosalia, he thought, a pretty name. He picked a blue flower from the side of the road and anguished that he had not thought to give it to her. He would head back. He would return to suffer her mother's anger.

He heard the car coming before it was upon him, angling in the soft dust and gravel. He did not want a ride, wanted to remain close to her, wanted to love. The sky was clear, agate blue, and it clutched at the pit of his stomach. The car guttered to a halt behind him, and with a resigned sigh he turned, his arm fanned wide for a lift.

The sheriff in a long tan cruiser motioned to Diego. Racing thoughts crowded his reason. *Small brown Mexican boy wanted. Arson. Murder. They had tracked him down,* he thought, *and this sheriff with bristling stubby grey hair would take him, cowering, guilty. There would be questions about the start, the horses, the smoke, the barn in flames. There would be the charred body. They would ask why, and he would have no answers. He would go to the big house and disappear.*

"Get over here," the sheriff commanded.

Though Diego felt his body poised for flight, his grip on his bag tight, his flapping shoes ready on his toes, he stood still. The engine purred. The sheriff leaned out the window, his arm snugged up against the car. "Boy?"

"*Sí?*" Diego's heart slammed in his chest, and a fine trembling took his breath away.

The man rapped his knuckles against the car. He stared at Diego's pack. "What you got in there?"

"Clothes, sandwiches," Diego muttered.

"Louder boy."

"Clothes. Sandwiches," Diego said, almost shouting.

The sheriff opened the car door from the outside and climbed out. He was tall. He hitched his tan trousers, scuffed the dusty earth. "You ain't hitchhiking?"

"No."

"No?"

"No, Sir."

"You up from around here?"

Diego swung his arm to indicate the long road ahead, hiding his feelings like water. "Gómez place."

"Gómez?" he said, staring into Diego's eyes. "You part of Rickie Gómez's clan?"

"*Sí.* My cousin. I visit."

"Should a said so from the get-go. I'll give you a ride. Hop in."

"No. No, Sir. I have bottles to find. Need to walk."

"There's bad blood in that family. They all carry knives." He stepped closer, lightly touching the gun in his holster. "You ain't carrying a knife?"

"No, Sir," and Diego backed away, unshouldering his pack. "Look. You see." He held his pack open.

"No need," the sheriff said, returning to the car, "but don't

118

let me catch you hitchhiking in this county. You get perverts and axmen and robbers. *Comprende.*"

"*Sí,*"

"Boy?" he said, turning again to face Diego.

"*Sí?*"

"You missed one," and his long shadow smothered Diego as he stooped to pick up a bottle and straightened to throw it across the road where it splintered and glittered in the noonday sun. He laughed then, his badge shimmering, the roar of it crashing through Diego's ears as the cruiser drove off.

Chapter 14:
Lubbock

Diego clutched the small matchbook where four matches remained. He would not waste them, not now, not so close to the law. He no longer looked for bottles, his mind alert for dangers. While kneeling at the side of the road, he had tied his mother's precious coins, and the dollars he had made in a soiled shirt and tucked them away in his bag when a semi roared up behind him. No one slowed or seemed to notice him hobbling alongside the road no matter how much he waved his arm. Blinded by fear, he seemed to lose direction, had lost the turn where Rosalia lived, could only recall her shy smile and sweet scent. He took out his map again knowing he would not make Lubbock by nightfall without a ride. He needed work to grow his dollars. Lubbock would be a sure thing, a large city or so it seemed on the map. He would invite the girl to see him sing. He would have that kiss. He would meet her mother, and she would not be angry that he was with her daughter.

When he hobbled into Spur, he stopped at a grocery and purchased a root beer, filled his empty orange Fanta bottle with water and looked for a place to sleep. Thinking of the girl had exhausted him. He wondered if he was near the Gómez place. He wandered the town for alleyways and finding nothing secretive enough, he walked out into the prairie. He settled behind a short rift of rock where he was hidden from the road. After eating the chicken sandwiches Effie had packed for him, his sack his pillow, he fell into an unsettled sleep.

"I am a man. See this, my Dolly," and his stepfather crushed the rattle-*snake's head beneath his boot. "It is trick to be brave like me," he laughed, the snake's tail writhing. Diego feared snakes. He tossed pebbles and grasses when he went into the prairie to start his fires, to scare them, but this man with his short, thick legs and his fat hands laughing, sneering, crying, "I should use this for whip. You like Diego?" made him cringe. "You no like? Then I give it to you anyway," and he flung the snake like a bullwhip until it lashed around Diego's neck. The boy screamed and slapped his head as if trying to hold onto his mind, and the squat stepfather laughed until the tears ran down his jowls.*

Diego woke hearing snakes all around him. He scrambled up on the rock leaving his bag. Stars glittered in the night sky. The moon was up, full and stern. Though the heat of the day remained in the rock, Diego shivered. The rattle sang on the scant wind, and he held his head as he had held it on that day. His teeth chattering, he spoke to himself.

"I'm not brave, but I am clever." He said this again and again, his hands loosening in his hair until he was weary and whispered, "I no think I am brave, but I am clever."

He sat up on the rock, the moon waning and saw his father smiling at him in the ghost shadows. He fell asleep sitting. When he woke with the dawn, he tossed the bag with his foot before gingerly picking it up.

He returned to the endless road, weary and hungry. *I must sing,* he thought, and began to murmur snatches of song randomly as if searching for a proper prayer. The night's scare hung with him. The car's raced past, his shoes beyond repair. He went into Spur again and bought jerky and a pair of blue, canvas shoes, white stars emblazoned on the blue, girl's shoes. The clerk laughed as he walked around the store in them. Diego tossed his road-worn shoes in a trash bin outside.

A truck was parked in the gravel outside of the store. Furniture and boxes of clothes and pans and jars sat in the open bed. Diego drank greedily from the hose on the side of the building; When a woman with two children, a boy and a girl, climbed into the truck Diego ran toward them.

"Missus, may I ride to Lubbock?"

She rolled her window halfway up.

"I am Pedro Gómez," Diego said trusting the smallness of the town. "Rickie Gómez is my uncle. I am his cousin."

The girl took interest and said, "I know Luciano Gómez. He's from my school," and she pinched her nose with her fingers and said, "He smells."

"That's enough," the woman said to the girl.

"He's very poor," Diego said in apology.

"We're all very poor around here. Rickie Gómez drinks."

"Yes, I know this. This is why I have come."

"You'll have to ride in back," she said, eyeing Diego's paint specked clothes.

"That is good," he said, turning quickly to the bed of the truck before she changed her mind.

The boy rolled down the other window and called to Diego.

"Carmina Gómez is in my class. She pees her pants."

"She shames her family. I will talk to her," he said, holding up his hands in abandon.

While the engine sputtered to life, Diego climbed into the back of the truck wedging himself between a box of clothes and an old porcelain pitcher, careful to not crush or break anything. Soon they were out on the highway, and Diego practiced whistling to add to his repertory of songs. He was confident he would find work in Lubbock.

The hour spent riding in the back of the truck, Diego thought about his luck. Some good, some bad. He had his money tucked away in his sack. Enough for a room perhaps, enough for a bath. He felt lucky about Lubbock. Maybe he would find his fortune there. He remembered the girl again. He would look for her once he got settled. *It was a fine day, hot and breezy, no clouds, dry as timber,* he thought, reaching for his matches.

As they entered Lubbock, the boy rapped on the rear window. The woman slowed the truck. It idled noisily as she got out.

"Lubbock. End of the line," she said, sweeping her arm to take in the expanse of street, the low buildings and watching Diego carefully as he leapt over the side of the truck, making sure he did not take anything.

"Thank you," he said. "I'll take the drink from Rickie. I promise."

She left him, the truck grumbling away, in the poor section of town. Bare boards covered windows. The glass in storefronts was soaped or painted 'CLOSED.' Children in raggedy clothes kicked the litter in the street to one another.

He walked swinging his bag, the coins clinking softly. As he came upon an abandoned lot wrapped around an auto repair shop, he gasped. Sitting in the lot was a brand new Ford Customline. It's metallic powder blue paint glinted in the sunlight. Hitchhiking, waiting for rides, he had seen but one of them, in Abilene, coursing down the highway, uncatchable, unmatched. It was sky blue, pure, untouched. Diego edged closer. Suddenly a youth, not much older than Diego, emerged from the repair shop.

"Paco, Paco," he called to Diego waving his arms.

"I am just looking. This is beauty."

"Damn straight it is," he said, unlocking the door.

"I have seen just one. Before, that is."

The boy, his face pocked with acne, his hair slicked back, a western hat cocked to one side of his head, said, "Come on, get in. I'll take you for a spin."

Diego couldn't believe his luck. He had hungered for a ride in such a vehicle for many miles, but the cars had never even slowed.

Once the boy was seated, he reached over and unlocked the passenger door. He motioned for Diego to climb in. Diego hesitated, suddenly aware of his sweat and dirty clothes.

The boy leaned over and rolled down the window. "You gettin' in or what?"

Diego clasped his sack to his belly, opened the door, and climbed in. The interior was even more impressive, slick vinyl seats, the dashboard, a myriad of dials and chrome.

"This yours?" Diego asked, finally catching his breath.

"Graduation present. My Pa never thought I'd make it. Something ain't it?"

"Sure. Inside and out, a beauty."

"Call her Ramona after my girl. You got a girl?"

"Yes. Back in Spur."

"That where ya from?"

"No. El Paso."

"Long way from home."

"Yes."

He turned the key in the ignition, and the car purred to life. The boy spun the tires, and the car lurched forward.

"Whoooee! This car can make time. Go Ramona!" and he careened onto the road and headed out a dirt lane that led off into the prairie. Diego said nothing, remembering how he tried to read the car makes as he walked waiting for a ride. Ford, Chevy. Trucks mostly. He watched the speedometer as it sped quickly up to forty, and fifty, and then seventy. Dust was flying everywhere. Rocks spun away from behind them. The car shimmied around curves, but Diego was not frightened.

Suddenly the boy braked, and the car spun and swerved and came to a stop on the grass.

"What do ya think?"

"Think speed ticket."

The boy laughed.

"What's that? What are ya carryin'?" The boy pointed at

Diego's bag.

"Clothes, bottles for money," Diego said, clutching his bag closer.

"No weapons or nothin'?"

"No."

The boy spun suddenly and ripped the bag from Diego's hand and upended it on the floor of the car. Soiled clothes, bottles, Diego's precious scraps of paper, the pot, the pants with his money tumbled out.

"No weapons? I'm particular about weapons," and he scooped up the can opener. "Could slice someone ear to ear with this," and he flung it in the back seat while rifling through the rest.

With one hand on the door, Diego pleaded. "No. Please?"

The boy reached across Diego to open the glove compartment. A pistol appeared in the boy's hand. He pressed it to the side of Diego's head. With his other hand, he shook the shirt that held his mother's coins, the pants that held his dollars. The money clattered and fluttered to the floor. The boy picked up the roll of dollars.

"Done pretty well for yourself," he said, tucking the wad of dollars in his shirt pocket, pressing the barrel at Diego's skull. "You wetbacks disgust me," and he turned just slightly to look out his rearview at a truck coming up the road. He lowered the gun for a second, and Diego grabbed the door handle and threw himself out of the car and scrambled into the brush. Diego ran, his heart pounding in his chest. Trees lined a narrow brook, and Diego splashed down the creek, slipping on rocks, crying. When the truck rumbled well past the boy's fancy car, Diego heard the gunshot that scared up the birds. He ran and ran, stumbling, blind with his tears. He stopped to catch his breath, to hear if he was being followed, then heard the Fairlane grumble into life speeding back down the lane.

Diego knelt on the ground. He felt for his matches, angrily recited his angel prayer, struck one, and lit the browned grass. Quickly the fire took. Bushes splintered in the fire, drooping branches caught. The splendor was too much: Diego stepped back, heedless that he was downwind, mindful only that he was lost. He stood rooted as the earth gave way to bright, orange flame.

He did not stay long enough to hear himself scream, a sudden softening, forgiving. He did not think to warn him. He did not warn him. He ran scared. He did not want the beating. He did not want to hear the stamp of the horse's hooves, their high, screaming whinny. He raced to the house, dusk falling fast, grabbing his mother's coins, his sack, his Diamond Tips and went racing across the prairie like a boy set afire.

The fire traveled quickly along the creek, the irrigation ditch, it did not matter, the brush and trees feeding it like a great ravaging animal. He sat there, the gentle breeze tugging at the fire until Diego's pants caught. He slapped it away gently like a child might pat the hand of his mother, petulant, uncertain. His skin burned, his canvas shoes turned black. When the rubber melted around his toes, he stood, a narrow opening in the engulfing fire. The fire crackled and popped as he picked his way, the fire, a halo, and made his escape.

Chapter 15:
The G.I.

Diego accepted rides like a whore. A day passed, maybe more. He looked for rides, his thumb out, with Oklahoma plates, asked to be let off when they noticed his limp, the smell of fire. He was dizzy with the fire, his foot throbbing, and when he was let off, he slept in the brush closed to traffic, to humanity.

He did not seek the ride. It was an offering. He no longer feared for his paltry life. He had no money, no food. The girl, Rosalia, had vanished from his thoughts. When the car stopped, an ordinary, dusty wagon, he climbed in, spoke little. He offered up Pedro Gómez in way of conversation. All he had was his map, burned where his pants had caught fire. He did not know where he was going. He did not care. His foot pained him, and his leg blistered. He knew only when the sirens had blared that he must go quickly.

The man driving had only one arm, the stump he leaned out the open window. The day was cloudy as if his fire had obliterated the sun. Diego waited for the story that would inevitably unfold. Diego did not expect kindness, nor did he plan to give it.

The man thrust a bag of potato chips he had on his lap toward him with his good arm.

"No. *Gracias,*" Diego said though he was hungry, though he was famished.

The man waved his stump to a fat, black woman who was walking. "She was my nurse. The arm," he waved it again, "you know."

They drove in silence for a few miles, the man steadying the steering wheel with his stump as he rifled the bag for potato chips, stuffing handfuls into his mouth as he drove. Diego hoped the man would turn on the radio to break the silence. "I've killed men. Lots of 'em. Got so close to the enemy I could smell what they had for breakfast." He laughed. "Got so close they blew off my arm. Scare you?" he waggled his stump.

"No," Diego said, his voice calm. "It is unlucky, yes, but no fear."

"Doctor says not to fear it. I don't 'cept whenever my fingers tingle. Can you beat that, my fingers lying on some Korean ridge tingling? Can you beat that?"

"No,"

"Go on touch it where the fingers might be. Two shots was all it took. Close range. I felt the wind kick up as it tore, still feel it sometimes. Two shots. Bled like a bitch. I was cryin' for Mama that's for sure. Go on."

Diego reached across the man, wagged his hand where the fingers might have been. The man watched Diego's face. Diego quickly drew in his hand.

"See? There. I can feel it. Ain't that somethin' now," he said, reaching for more potato chips. "Doc says it's nerves that don't want to quit. Ain't that something to slice a man's arm and still have it live? Oh, I've killed plenty. Bad war."

He crumpled the empty bag on his lap and threw it on the floor. "Custom made the clutch high on the column, so I let go, shift, hold. It's one quick motion. I drive like a saint, don't worry."

They drove again in silence, and Diego was about to ask if he could put on the radio when the man said, "You ever kill anything?" Diego remained silent. "Coyote? Hen? Anything?"

"No, Sir."

"I like that. Sir. Sounds like I'm talking to my sergeant. The good ol' days. You know what I mean?"

He paused, looking around his seat. He picked up the package of Lucky Strikes, tapped one out on the steering wheel, and put it in his mouth. "You got a light?"

"No, Sir."

"There's that sir again. I kind of like it. Like I was sayin', if you haven't killed a thing, then you haven't properly lived. You got an enemy whether it's a coyote in your henhouse or a man with a gun, you kill. It's as natural as the morning is long. You got to kill to live, how I figure it. Tomatoes, corn or a thick, juicy steak. Ain't that right, kid?" The unlit cigarette bobbed on his lips.

"Sure," Diego answered, but he was not sure at all.

"Dolly!" he barked. "Diego!" The barn door slammed shut. Fire hissed.

"You can let me out here," Diego said breathlessly.

"Nah, you wanted to go on to…"

"I've change my mind."

"Scares you, don't it?" and he wiggled the remaining shoulder, the remaining stump. "I seen where they left my arm. The medic didn't think to carry it away. What am I gonna do with it anyway? Frame it over the fireplace?"

"No. Here," Diego pointed, his breath short, rasping.

"The mountains is the worst. Snow, cold, armed men," he said whiping over to the side of the road. "Armed men, now that's a joke on me," he said, waving his stump. "Have yourself a day now."

Chapter 16:
Sister Mary Joseph

He staggered in the middle of the road, his foot festering and rising out of the canvas shoe. He walked in the middle of the road. A sign appeared. Welcome to Oklahoma.

He sensed something was wrong, some misdirection, some trick. He hobbled over to the sign, leaned against it, feverish, rubbing his hands along it. *I have not planned to leave Texas*, he thought groggily. A car veered away behind him, stopped. It was a hallucination, a black dream. His body lurched forward to be sick, but only a thin stream of bile trickled down his chin. Someone grabbed his elbow, then circled an arm around his back. "Are you sick?" she asked, her voice brusque.

Diego scrambled for words, English words, but he had none.

"Come," she said, and she led him to the car, stiffly pushed him in, lifted his legs, and then he screamed. "You're hurt. Rattlesnake?" she said, noting his swollen foot. Diego shook his head. She felt his forehead. Her black habit shrouded her slight frame. She looked like a small, dark chapel, and Diego got into the car without words.

"You're burning up," she said, passing her hand across his fore-head and quickly and quietly pulled the car onto the road. "You need a hospital." Diego thrashed and shook his head violently.

"No."

"You'll come with me then."

Diego heard nothing more until two rough hands were pull-ing him out of the car, until his clothes were stripped from him, until his shoes with the stars were removed. He slept throughout the afternoon and into the night. When he awoke, the moonlight illuminated a roomful of cots, small cries issued from the lump of bodies sleeping. He fell back asleep. He awoke again to the smell of corn cakes frying and a painful throbbing in his foot.

The nun that had picked him up hovered over him with a plate. "When did you eat last?"

"Yesterday, maybe the day before."

"Then eat this." Diego sat up embarrassed with his naked chest, the scars. He pulled the thin blanket over his shoulders, took the offered plate, and wolfed the corn cakes with sweet molasses.

"You are lucky. The doctor makes his visit today. He will look at your foot, the burns. He will know what to do. You should be in a hospital. You are lucky."

Diego did not look up. He did not want to stare at those green eyes, the pallid face, the mysterious blackness that surrounded her, the cane she leaned on. He had experience with Sister Ann Luke at the mission. Stern and unfriendly, quick with a stick.

"I am Sister Mary Joseph," she said, taking the empty plate. "I run the orphanage here at San Miguel. We have mostly boys. Run-aways," she said, turning slightly, waving to the sleeping bodies. "I can sense a runaway, the way he skitters from human touch, the way he holds his head, the way he smells," she paused. "You smell. Where are you from?"

Diego had never lied to the stern and unfriendly sisters at the mission, had only omitted the shaming things in confession to Fa-ther Felipe. He had been where he had been, had seen what he had seen, he could not fathom lying now.

"El Paso."

"Phew. Never has a boy traveled that far, a few miles, yes, the next county, but not so far. Well, we will talk about all of this later, once you've bathed, once the doctor has seen you. Can you walk?"

"*Sí*," and he wrapped the blanket around him and hobbled, his foot flaming, after Sister Mary Joseph.

"You will find clothes there," and she pointed with her cane to a narrow wooden bench, "and towels and soap in there. Clean those burns well," and she swept around, her skirt rustling, and tapped tapped out of the room.

He welcomed the warm water. He soaped his hair, and the water turned brown as it swam down his body. His foot was red and angry, but he scrubbed it anyway, screaming silently. His toes were blackened, and he feared the doctor would remove them. He would find a way of escape, though he had no matches, no dollars, none of his mother's coins. He did not know what day of the week it was. The doctor would not come on a Sunday. He would stay until Sunday. He would steal a few coins from the collection plate. He would leave. He would find matches.

Diego felt awkward in the mission clothes. They smelled of sand and soap powder. He missed Millie's husband's trousers. He missed his burlap sack. He felt naked when he was finally faced with Sister Mary Joseph's questions. They sat in a little alcove outside of the sacristy, she at a desk, he in the chair beside her, bibles and ancient hymnals behind her on a bookshelf.

"Did your parents leave those marks?" Diego squirmed in his chair.

"No, my Mama and Papa would not harm me."

"Then who?"

"My Papa was a good man, always smiling, laughing with others, with me. Although he prepared coffin nails, he did not die. He left. One day he was on a rooftop howling, and next, he is gone. Mama would not tell me."

"You are scarred on your back and chest. I cannot send you

home to such a brute. Tell me. Who?"

"My stepfather do this. He is, as you say, brute. But he is gone."

"Gone where?"

"I cannot tell. I make a confession today. It's enough."

"The priest is away. He will not be back until Sunday. You can make your confession then." She opened the desk drawer and took out a small, beaded rosary. "Here. Thank God that you are alive," and she handed the rosary to Diego. "You know I do not even know your name."

"Diego Ramírez." He had grown fond of Pedro Gómez, how the name had saved him from scrapes, from danger, from intimacy, but he could not lie to that pale face, those green eyes, the wooden cross hanging down on her chest.

"Can I have shoes?"

"I do not issue shoes to runaways until I have reason to suspect they will not run again. I suspect you are the running kind. Besides, your foot is still swollen and festering. That is enough for now. As I said, the priest will hear your confession Sunday."

Diego had lost track of days.

"What day is this?"

"It is Monday. Although I cannot give you absolution, I am here if you wish to talk."

"No, I'll save it for the priest."

"Very well, then. The doctor will see you after lunch," and she shut the drawer, took up her cane, and waited until Diego rose and walked unsteadily down the corridor.

While Diego waited for the doctor to come, he played marbles with the boys, played cat's cradle with the girls. The boys marveled at the scars on his legs, the festering foot, baring their own, believing themselves heroes. They complained about the food, the hard cots, but spoke little of their escapades that ended up at the mission.

"Sister Mary Joseph is strict," one boy said.

"She eats nails," another replied. They laughed and snickered and hid their hands behind their backs or crossed their arms tightly around their waists.

When the doctor arrived, they scattered. The doctor was built like a pyramid, small, pointed head, bushy eyebrows, black spectacles. Triangular, his shoulders narrowed and spread to his waist, weighted with a broad beam, and wide legs, and flat feet. "Dr. Jaris Hopkins." The man offered his hand.

"Diego Ramírez," he said, his name sounding foreign. He did not take the man's hand.

"Let's look at that burn."

"No burn."

"Whatever you say. Let's take a look at it anyway."

Diego sat back on the cot, stuffing the pillow across his chest.

"This may hurt, probably will hurt," the doctor cautioned as he opened his black bag and set it next to Diego. "When did this happen?" he asked and spread the charred toes, skin peeling away in thick black crusts.

Diego did not scream. He bit his lip, hugged the pillow.

"There was fire a few mornings back in Lubbock, ran up along an irrigation creek. Did you get caught up in it?"

"No," Diego said quickly. "I didn't see a fire."

"Was a bad one. No one reported injured, no burns, so I guess all's right with the world, 'cept this.

"*Sí.*"

"Well, good then," the doctor said. "You're to keep off this foot for a week. No shoes, no socks. Let it air. I'll give Sister Mary Joseph ointment to apply three times a day. Keep it clean. We'll see if you're going to keep those toes or not. Even if they do heal, they're going to be pinched and tight, but I suspect they won't hinder you from walking," the doctor straightened, snapped his black case shut, and began to turn. "You were lucky this time," he said, peering under his bushy eyebrows, "You may not be so lucky the next." The man walked to the door where Sister Mary Joseph was standing. They talked quietly, and then he turned to Diego again,

"I'll see you in four days," and he left.

Sister Mary Joseph came into the room, children hovered nearby, listening.

"Dr. Hopkins said there was a fire. I pray to God for your soul. You are to rest. There will be no playing. If it is not too hot, you may sit outside. I will get a chair and an umbrella to shade your leg. The children will look up to you. I forbid you to talk with them about where you have been or where you are going. Is that clear?"

"*Sí.*"

Diego waited for the doctor, waited for the priest, waited for his confession. He sat outside, an umbrella propped over his bare foot, his head throbbing where the gun had been held. He was restless, and the Sister humored him with books and newspapers. He saw the photograph of his fire, and inwardly he railed that it was not big enough, not angry enough, had not damaged enough. The orphans had been instructed to leave him alone, but one little girl braved her way to his side.

"What happened to your foot?"

"A tiger ate it," and he whooped in mock pain, bared his teeth and laughed, and she ran away.

He read words Arson. Lubbock. Fire. He felt pride swell his chest then remembered the words he would share with the priest and fell silent, thumbing the book pages, restless.

When Dr. Hopkins returned, Diego's foot had faded to a raw pink, his toes cherry red.

Sister Mary Joseph accompanied the doctor, tap tapping her way to his bed.

"Is he ready for work?" she asked.

"Yes. I think he is. You will not lose those toes, but you will limp for a while, maybe forever. Time will tell," and he packed up his black case and left the orphanage. Sister Mary Joseph followed the doctor to his car then returned to Diego's side.

"The doctor has given more ointment. It is still several days until Father Benito will return. The doctor says you may work. I have much work here, and you will help. You may start by helping the cook with the breakfast dishes."

"Shoes?" Diego asked.

"A sock will do," and she rummaged in a pile of laundry on the next bed and pulled out a sock.

"Here."

Diego grimaced in pain as he pulled the sock over his burnt foot and limped into the kitchen. He scrubbed pots and pans, plates, knives and spoons. When he was done, Sister Mary Joseph had him carry in groceries from the delivery truck and put them meticulously away. Lunch was served in the common room. Diego ate fiercely, then Sister Mary Joseph ordered him back into the kitchen to wash dishes again. Then there was laundry, dinner, and more dishes.

Diego, exhausted, fell into a dreamless sleep.

Sister Mary Joseph woke him with her cane.

"Father Benito will hear your confession after mass. You are to see that all the children are washed and dressed by nine."

"Sister?" Diego said as she was turning. "What is Father Benito like?"

"He is strict," she said, thumping her cane. "We have children to look after, so he is strict."

Diego rounded up the children, shoving the older boys into the shower, having the girls prepare their Sunday dresses, raggedy but clean. There was much commotion, pushing, yelling, but by nine Diego had them all scrubbed and dressed when Sister Mary Joseph came to fetch them.

Diego pleaded again for a shoe, but she only glared at him.

She motioned them into the church with her cane and assigned them benches. Diego sat in the aisle seat close to the altar. Parishioners filed in slowly, lit votive candles, and sat. They, too, were dressed poorly, but they were clean. Diego was fascinated by the candles, the warm light they shed, the flickering of hope.

Father Benito had thick black hair, a firm jaw, and a resonant voice. He held onto the altar as if for support and willed the congregation for forgiveness. He read from the scriptures.

"And the angel of the Lord appeared unto him in a flame of fire out of the midst of a bush: and he looked, and, behold, the bush burned with fire, and the bush was not consumed," he paused before reading on and looked over where the children were seated, and it seemed to Diego that Father Benito looked right through him. Diego did not know *consumed*, but the softening of the priest's eyes, seemed to suggest hope, so he listened and thought no more of his confession.

While the mass continued, the last of the congregation taking communion, Diego stepped up to the altar. He took the wafer in his mouth, hoping to feel the body of Christ, but gagged on the wafer dissolving on his tongue. He waved the altar boy away and made for the back of the church. Sister Mary Joseph stood, slightly bent over, both hands on her cane.

"Father Benito does not like to be kept waiting. There," she said pointing to the confessional with her cane, and Diego had no recourse, there was no ride out of here, even his thumb would not help.

The confessional gleamed as if recently polished. He opened the door and knelt on the kneeler.

"Forgive me, Father for I have sinned."

A raspy breath called, "And what of your sins?"

"I have set fire. Many times. I think I killed a man."

"What man?"

"My stepfather," he paused, and then he told him every detail of that afternoon, the beatings, how he touched him like a hateful dog, how he had decided it was the end of things, how his stepfather called to him, "Dolly! Dolly!" and how his outrage had burst like the Rio Grande in spring. He told how he had taken his soiled pants, soaked them with kerosene, and set them against the dry, splintered boards of the barn; how he had never set fires so close to home before. He told him how he had lit them with his Diamond Tips, how alive he had felt then, strong, and when he saw his stepfather step into the barn, he reveled, he laughed, he was high on evil, but he thought quickly and made his plans, and then he was on the road. It happened like that, like a prairie hen startled.

"Is he dead?"

"I don't know."

"Did you read it in the papers?"

"I read poor."

"Then you assume he's dead?"

"*Sí*," he whispered.

"There are not enough Hail Marys or Our Fathers to recite to undo this sin. There are not enough rosary beads."

"*Sí*," Diego's voice broke.

"To kill is a grievous sin. Perhaps your stepfather lives, perhaps not, but you meant to take his life whatever the outcome, that is the sin," the priest's robes stirred. "Tomorrow, we bury a man, a poor man, a man not unlike your stepfather, a man brutal with his family, so he has no one now to say a prayer at his funeral. You will dig his grave, light a candle at his service, you will kiss the man's lips, you will throw the first soil onto his grave, and you will sing a mourning prayer for him. You will see death first hand. I want you to think about this man, your stepfather, reason with him, feel pity for him, but refuse to hate him. I will be gone in the morning but will be back later in the day for the funeral. Sister Mary Joseph will oversee your penance. Go with God."

Diego was agitated. He wanted to be absolved at once, wanted his stepfather, his voice, to stop circling in his mind. *Wasn't the world a better place without him*, he thought. How often he had tried to erase him, how often he had come creeping back.

My dolly. My dolly.

Sister Mary Joseph met him on the church steps, a shovel in hand. She marked out the grave, scraping her cane in the dust.

"He's not a big man. He won't have a coffin," then she looked up at the sky. "You'd better start."

Diego wondered how much the priest had told her, and as if reading his thoughts, she said, "Digging a grave is hard penance," then grim-faced, she turned and walked back to the church.

The earth was hard, brittle, and Diego could only use the one foot to shovel the dirt. Diego cursed the drought. He dug and dug. A child lingered near the site, his thumb in his mouth, watching. Diego refused to talk, and eventually, the child wandered off. Blood blisters rose on his hands and burst, and as he wiped his brow of sweat, blood streaked his forehead. There was fierceness about him as slowly the pile of dirt grew large. He stood in the grave up to his waist, sweat glistening on his face and arms, his clothes soaked through. His mind was gratefully blank.

His voice was loud, booming, unlike the soft cajoling voice of his father. It had struck the seven-year-old Diego, that the voice, so foreign, was welcome. The silence after his father had disappeared, his sisters' silences, his mother's tears, had frightened him, so much so, that he had taken to sleeping on the burlap sack, filled with rags, that had been his father's pillow. He would empty the sack during the day and carry it with him, curling it about his shoulders, tying it about his waist. The man, standing on the porch with his booming voice, had laughed at him.

"What's your name?"

"Diego," he had answered. The man laughed more, louder.

"My dolly. In English you will be my dolly."

Sister Mary Joseph came with lunch and a glass of water. "Another foot," she remarked then drew away.

When he stood in the grave up to his heart, he knew it was finished. He climbed out, carried the shovel back inside, and went to the dormitory where he collapsed on his cot. Sister Mary Joseph brought him supper, but he could not eat. She set the plate on the floor beside his bed and sat down next to him.

"Father Benito has gone to perform extreme unction. An old man will die tonight. He is very ill. You will bury him tomorrow after mass. He will die a very old, bitter man. You will kiss his dead lips. You will say a prayer for his soul. You will throw the dirt on his grave," she sighed. "You are young and already so old. I pray for your soul."

She rose to leave, the bed creaked, her cane found purchase on the floor. "Diego Ramírez, you will face this. Father Benito does not make mistakes."

Diego felt a crushing sadness. He tossed and turned, but he could not sleep. He watched the moon spread across the dormitory, heard the cries of the orphaned boys. When the sun rose to wake him, he was wide-eyed and staring. Sister Mary Joseph came to him early.

"Wash and dress, then see to the little ones. The man has died. The children will be the only ones to attend. Go now. Hurry."

The blood in his foot pounded, but he washed and dressed and saw to the children. Breakfast was meager, a bowl of porridge, but Diego lapped it up eagerly. Sister Mary Joseph gathered the children, and they filed out of the dormitory and into the church. After they were seated, two men carried a body wrapped in a faded green blanket to a waiting table near the altar.

They pulled away the blanket that covered the dead man's face. He was dressed in the faded garb Diego recognized as the man's work clothes. The men walked back to the church's entrance and stood, their long shadows striking the aisle. Sister Mary Joseph nodded to Diego.

He rose, his steps faltering until he could smell the garlic the dead man had eaten, the whiskey he had drunk. The man's face was marbled with purple, and his thick lips were the color of the dark night. Faint, Diego wobbled on his bad foot. He leaned over the dead man's face. His belly churned. He looked up. Sister Mary Joseph nodded. The children murmured. She called for silence. Diego bent down, his lips brushing the man's black mustache, his lips.

He wanted to call out, to be rescued, but he was a man. He had to do these things to be absolved, *that was what Father Benito had said, wasn't it*, he thought. He leaned in again, placed his lips against the man's, felt the dampness as if for a moment the man had lived, had taken a sip of water only moments before. And as Diego kissed him, he felt the fleetingness of life, the quiver of blood in the dead man's veins, the void of death. A child giggled.

He straightened and walked to the table of candles. None had been lit. The priest took his place in front of the altar. He watched Diego, and Diego's hands trembled. He took up a wooden match from a bowl and struck it against a striker. It flared and then weakened and went out. He took another one, struck it, and it held. He lowered his face over the glass, touched the flame to the wick. He felt no hunger. The priest nodded to Sister Mary Joseph and began the mass.

Diego sat on the front bench trying to listen, but his head was full of questions. *Would a bad man go to heaven, would he no longer be driven, would he endlessly run.* The men of shadows arrived. Mass was over. Sister Mary Joseph appeared with the shovel as the man was carried to the grave. The priest followed Diego out of the church.

"Have you prepared your mourning words?"

"*Sí.*"

Diego took the shovel and threw the dirt into the grave. The priest nodded.

Diego knew of two sins, brutality and death. He struggled for words, for prayer, and settled with satisfaction on his guardian angel prayer, his summons for fire. In a voice, sweet with remorse and revenge, he recited as if it were a song, a lullaby.

"Oh my dear Angel Guardian, preserve me from the misfortune of offending God."

The priest nodded again. The sounds, the words spoken in the sweltering sun, a sun-like fire, washed over the meager mourners.

"Eternal rest grant unto them, O Lord, and let perpetual light shine upon them. May the souls of the faithful departed, through the mercy of God, rest in peace. Amen."

The children, who were gathered on either side of the grave whispered, "Amen."

Sister Mary Joseph and the priest and Diego, in unison, solemnly murmured, "Amen."

They stood there, the children, the priest, Sister Mary Joseph, and Diego as if waiting for something to happen, for some sign: and then the priest sighed and motioned everyone inside.

Diego started to fill in the grave. He did this hurriedly, trying to escape the fierce sun, the man's eyes which peered out at him from the green blanket. His foot no longer mattered. He could not feel pain, would not feel pain. He threw the earth again and again. The body began to disappear, but Diego could not bring himself to cover the man's eyes. He stared into them. The priest had said he was a brutal man, like his stepfather, but the eyes were brown like his own, and he could not break his gaze. He felt a stirring in his chest.

He knew them, the new boys on the ranch, eager to be useful, eager for food and pay. He followed them sometimes into the barn, along the fences, into the prairie. The leader was Juan, small and lithe, a fast runner, an able worker. He was a boy younger and handsomer than Diego.

When he saw them together, his thick-legged stepfather and the boy, Juan's face shining eager to please; when he saw his stepfather put his arm around the boy's shoulder, talking into his ear, the jealousy drowned him. He threw his bucket at the boy, hit his shin, and the boy yelped and ran off. His stepfather only smiled.

He felt no joy in the sun, in the dead man's eyes, and he buried his legs and then his chest. The dead man's eyes questioned him even in their dull blank stare. Carrying small shovelfuls of dirt, he filled in the spaces about the man's face. Gently he threw dirt on the man's chin. Then, as if the man might sit bolt upright and cry "No!" he covered the man's face. When he was finished, when the man no longer stared, no longer questioned, when he was buried, dead and gone, Diego stamped on the grave, tamping the dirt, unaware of the shooting pain in his foot. He jabbed the shovel into the earth and went to seek Sister Mary Joseph. "I need shoes."

"You can stay. We have a school here. Father Benito has suggested it."

"I am not a orphan."

"Where will you go?"

"To El Paso."

"Home?"

"*Sí.*"

"If you really mean to go home," she said, hiding her disappointment, "you will need some money." She reached into her habit pocket and pulled out some bills. She handed them to Diego. "There is enough for a bus ticket to El Paso."

"*Gracias,*" he said tucking the dollars away.

"A bus leaves from Goodwell at two forty-five. It travels through many towns. You will not be tempted to stop?"

"No, Sister."

"If I give you shoes, you will not be tempted to run?"

"No."

"Good then, let us get you some shoes," and they entered the dormitory. There was a closet full to overflowing with dresses, pants, socks, undershirts, and shoes. A parcel lay on the floor, and Sister Mary Joseph picked it up and opened it.

"These should fit. Try them on."

Diego sat down on the floor and pulled on a worn pair of work boots. He stood, stamped his feet, and declared, "They fit. They are fine."

"They are the dead man's shoes. I think you will wear them well." She turned, shutting the closet door. "I cannot give you a ride into town. The children. You must promise me you will not hitchhike. Promise?"

"*Sí.*"

The church lane was a broken road. He walked one step, two steps, out toward the main highway. He had lied to a nun, something he had never done. The boots did not fit. His scorched toes bounced up and down, and he knew before he got into town he would be covered with new blisters. Once he was out on the highway, he would catch a ride, his promise to her broken. A dead man's shoes. A brutal man's shoes. He did not walk comfortably, and his back was sore from digging. She would understand. Once the church was out of sight, he thrust out his arm. Cars and trucks sailed by, and he made little progress walking. He could still see the rutted church lane.

Finally, as he struggled forward, a brown sedan stopped.

"You need a ride?" the man called.

"Yes." And Diego hobbled over to the car door and climbed in.

"Bad foot?"

"Very bad," and Diego laughed.

The man wore shiny black trousers with a clean white shirt. He was thick-legged and wore polished black shoes. His gut sprouted out of his waistband as he twisted the car onto the road.

"Where you goin'?

"Into town."

"You from the orphanage?"

"Yes," Diego replied reluctantly.

"Orphan?"

"No."

"Feel sorry for them kids."

Dangling from the dashboard was a photograph of two boys held by a thread taped beneath the rearview mirror. He noticed Diego looking at them.

"Robby and Will," the man said. Good boys. One's a football player, the other an oil man. This photo is old. Real old," and he laughed. "You a good boy?"

Diego thought of his absolution and then of his lies. "I

suppose."

"Good. I don't like bad boys," and he clutched Diego's crotch.

Diego swung around and yanked the steering wheel. The car lurched off the road into the brush and sped toward a great wall of rock. A great crashing of rock and chrome splintered the air. Diego flew into the dashboard. Blue smoke flowed from the engine. He felt his face. The man next to him groaned. The photograph of the two boys swung madly. Diego pulled on the doorknob. The door wouldn't open, and he dragged his feet up from the floor and threw himself out the open window. He ran around the other side of the car.

"Get out!" he shouted to the man.

Fire leaped out of the front of the car. Diego ran down the road dragging his injured foot.

"Get out!" he shouted again.

"I'm stuck. Help!"

"My Dolly!"

"You pig. Die!" and Diego turned and headed once again for town. He muttered to himself, "I wish not to do this. I am sin. Forgive me." He concentrated on walking.

It was payday. He had been in town, spending his money on sweet beer. He had come into the room roaring.

"Constantina, Esmerelda, Almira!" His pockets were full as he stood before them. Diego came in behind him, squirmed and twisted to avoid his touch and watched as he handed out his gifts. A rope bracelet for his mother, a hairbrush for Esmerelda, a pretty blond doll for Almira. He stared at Diego with dead eyes. Diego was prepared to run before he could take him to the back room.

"Diego" he cried hoarsely, and he threw a small blue and white pack-age to Diego. It was candy. Diego held it to his nose. Chocolate. He was greedy for it but saw his stepfather's cruel smile and flung it to the floor.

"Help. I'm on fire."

"Dolly? My Dolly?"

Confused, Diego saw the dead man's eyes, the one he had buried. He ran toward the flaming car. He struggled with the door and pulled the man out of the car and dragged him to the side of the road. He would be seen here. Cars would pass. Someone would stop. Someone would see him. Someone would stop. He could not explain. He hurried as fast as he was able to town. He was not absolved. It would take some time, a lifetime perhaps. He felt old.

He purchased his ticket in silence, pointing to the town on the schedule, offering up Sister Mary Joseph's dollars. He walked uncertainly to the stop. The sign above the bus window read: Amarillo, Lubbock, Odessa, El Paso. He showed the ticket he had purchased and climbed on. The bus was full, and he sat in a seat behind some boys who were traveling with their grandmother.

"How long will it be?"

"Will we get ice cream?"

"Will Pappy pick us up?"

Their innocence was contagious, and Diego felt for his matchless pocket, thought absently of his own father, leaned over the seat as they did, peering out the great glass window as the bus roared to life.

The Ride
Discussion Questions

1. What kind of boy is Diego?

2. Is Diego guilty of murder?

3. What kind of relationship does Diego have with his family? His sisters, his mother, his father, his stepfather?

4. How does singing change Diego?

5. Why does he refuse to leave Texas?

6. What would it be like to be an illiterate youth in an English speaking world?

7. Why does he pray before he sets his fires?

8. How does Diego cope with the world, the drivers, the abuse?

9. Which drivers help Diego the most?

10. At the end of the book does Diego go home or some where else? Why?

CPSIA information can be obtained
at www.ICGtesting.com
Printed in the USA
FFHW020416150219
50550341-55860FF